# ONCE A RANGER

'Once a ranger, always a ranger' — so the saying went. But when Clint Taggart left under pressure, he was never happier. Then tragedy struck and the rangers wanted him back. Against his better judgement, he agreed and found his life and that of his remaining family in unimaginable danger: up against the biggest threat Texas had ever seen! But he still retained the old Ranger training, and Clint rode to meet his enemies head-on, determined to face the consequences.

HANK J. KIRBY

# ONCE A RANGER

*Complete and Unabridged*

**LINFORD**
*Leicester*

First published in Great Britain in 2007 by
Robert Hale Limited
London

First Linford Edition
published 2008
by arrangement with
Robert Hale Limited
London

British Library CIP Data

Kirby, Hank J.
    Once a ranger.—Large print ed.—
Linford western library
1. Texas Rangers—Fiction
2. Western stories 3. Large type books
I. Title
823.9'2 [F]

ISBN 978–1–84782–470–7

Published by
F. A. Thorpe (Publishing)
Anstey, Leicestershire

Set by Words & Graphics Ltd.
Anstey, Leicestershire
Printed and bound in Great Britain by
T. J. International Ltd., Padstow, Cornwall

This book is printed on acid-free paper

# 1

## Night Fire

Altogether, they set nine fires, seven in and around the town and two at the stockyards.

Naturally, with all nine starting within minutes of each other and being spotted early by various citizens and soldiers from the fort, the big alarm bell in the plaza began to clang furiously. People ran in all directions, banging on doors, shouting warnings, essentially the same each time:

'The town's on fire! Get out and save yourselves!'

Other men, more practical, bellowed:

'Start a bucket line! Get down to the creek with everything that'll hold water — or the town'll burn down around your ears!'

The sense of panic brought results,

although chaos reigned for the first twenty minutes, folk tripping over each other, screaming the names of family members they couldn't immediately locate. The fort was emptied of soldiers in various stages of dress and undress, barefoot, bare-chested, one man wearing only his long johns. These were soon saturated with water spilled from the pails passing hand to hand and clung revealingly to his skinny body. A red-faced lieutenant screamed at the man to go make himself decent, adding, 'You're on report as of this moment!'

The soldier muttered under his breath, jog-trotted back to the barracks, then decided that, seeing as the place was entirely deserted, why the hell hurry? In fact, why bother going back at all? The whole blame town was out, fighting the fires; if they couldn't extinguish them, then his being there wasn't going to make any difference.

*Now, where had that loud-mouth loot stashed the keys to the medicine cabinet that held the emergency brandy?*

The fires had taken hold on the weather-dry timber buildings. Flickering amber light, shot through with bursts of bright red as flames spurted in lashing tongues from more inflammable materials, turned the scene into something that might be glimpsed through the gates of hell.

People tended to take care of their own property, which was natural enough, but there was a squad of hard-faced soldiers under a baccy-chewing sergeant doing the rounds who literally dragged these persons back to the main fires.

'Save the town, you idiots! No town, it ain't worth even tryin' to rebuild! Git back to Main, damn you! Judas, Kelly, that blame hovel of yours ain't worth savin'! Move now or I'll gunwhip you myself! Magill, goddammit! Leave that sideboy. Aw, for Chrissakes, Corporal, prod 'em with your bayonet! Dumb bastards won't move otherwise!'

There would be complaints and

repercussions afterwards, but time enough then to worry about such things.

The flames were spreading. Smoke was choking, hacking at throats, searing eyes, making already terrified children scream even louder, cling to their mothers' sodden, mud-spattered skirts, causing adults to trip up.

Down by the railway siding, a couple of hundred yards from the end of Main Street, a train was sitting, occasionally illuminated by brightly flaring buildings as roofs collapsed. There were four cars behind the locomotive, while warming coals glowed beneath the boiler in the engineer's cab, keeping it ready for an early start come morning.

This was the train from the armory out at Arlington, back along the track from Dallas. It had been loaded with a hundred cases of brand-new Sharps Cavalry carbines, in .45–70 government-calibre, centrefire, with an improved graduated sight and the solid safety device of a half-cock hammer. It was a standard weapon for Frontier

4

Cavalry units and had been used by the Seventh Cavalry at Little Big Horn as well as Trapdoor Springfields. Though many attacking Sioux had repeaters, the Sharps, a single-shot with a falling-block breech action which allowed a competent soldier to fire off seven to ten shots a minute, gave a good account of itself — until ammunition ran out. Keep the ammunition coming to fifty, a hundred, soldiers and you had a devastating force against any enemy. But no ammo — then prepare to die, soldier boy!

The guns had been field-tested with massively destructive results against the Sioux and Comanche and were now being shipped to the South-West where the Apache menace was looming under several chiefs who had combined forces.

One of the locked box-cars contained nothing but ammunition and spares. The whole shipment was due to leave before sun-up on its long journey to the scattered forts, which were unable to cope with the latest murderous Apache raids.

But there were men who had other ideas about the destination of these fine firearms. The same men who had set the fires all over town.

There were a dozen of them, mainly Mexican: hardened gun-runners and thieves, men who would kill without compunction, men experienced in all aspects of this planned robbery, laying the fires in the most strategic parts of the town, set to ignite by slowburn fuses in the business sections *and* the residential areas. The stockyards happened to be crammed with steers, ready for the meatworks train due to arrive within the next couple of days.

There was every indication now that when it did come, it would find most of its intended cargo already barbecued . . .

Two of the men, who were making their way towards the darkened train, turned off towards the stockyards where the bellowing of the terrified steers drowned out everything except the

6

occasional roar as a wall or roof collapsed.

Men were working on the fires around the pens, sweating and staggering under slopping pails of creek water, fighting to extinguish the flames that were desperately trying to take hold on the posts, rails and gates of the pens; if they burned through the herds would be let loose.

Then there would be a stampede and those sections of town that had so far escaped damage by the fires would stand a very good chance of being flattened and destroyed as fear-mad animals smashed through doors and street-front windows and even the flimsy walls, or knocked down awning support posts.

So the gun-runners drew their pistols and began picking off the fire-fighters, the gunfire drowned by the thundering chaos in the town. Two men went down and then someone started shooting back, yelling that they were under attack.

More of the firefighters, those who were armed, anyway, dropped their pails and ran to help. Bullets whined and ricocheted, men were running and shooting from crouched positions, there being not much cover on offer. The gun-runners called for back-up and three more men ran up from the train area.

A man was shot from the top corral rail as he tried to draw a bead on one of the attackers. He fell amongst the cows and even if the bullet hadn't finished him, the stomping hoofs and raking horns did the job.

'Turn 'em loose!' someone yelled. 'Turn the damn critters loose!'

'Kill these sons of bitches!' cried one of the townsmen. 'They're tryin' to start a stampede!'

His words choked off as one of the raiders put a bullet in the man's chest and he toppled backwards. Then someone knocked the first rail down. It hit with a ringing thud, quickly followed by another, and then the gun-runner had to leap for his life as the first of the cattle surged through the gap. Horns clashed, raked hides and fences, the weight forcing the posts to lean at an angle until they cracked or tore loose from the earth.

Then a veritable river of cattle burst out and thundered into the night, the fires reflecting from white, rolling eyes and long, twitching horns . . .

At the train, the few soldiers who were left on guard-duty despite the burning town, came awake at last and grabbed their guns. Other guns cracked and spat fire into the smoky night, cutting the guards down mercilessly.

'Mel!' a voice bawled. 'How's the loco?'

'Pressure's almost there, Mitch!'

'Hurry it up!'

'Can't. Got to let it build at its own speed.'

Mitch swore, then yelled again. 'I said, hurry it up!'

It was another ten minutes before the gauge showed the level of pressure that suited Mel, once a railroad man who had been sent to Yuma penitentiary for aiding train-robbers by selling them confidential schedules. Now he was ready, cut in the steam to the drive pistons, nodded to the waiting Mexican fireman to start shovelling more coal under the boilers. He automatically reached for the whistle cord but snatched his hand back in time: no sense in alerting the townsmen. It would give 'em a nice dilemma though: save the guns or save the town!

Mel knew what he'd do but his job right now was to get this damn train rolling — and fast.

Which he did, clanking the couplings as a warning to his fellow-thieves that they were ready to roll. Men came swarming on to the train and into the caboose, a couple jumping on to the footplates of the driver's cab.

Shooting sparks into the already spark-laden night, with thick, foggy smoke swirling and blotting out the stars, the arms train chugged out of the siding, belching its own roiling black column of smoke. It began to gather speed, the throbbing note of the locomotive rising and thudding as it streaked across the prairie away from the burning town and the dead men. From somewhere in the night came the fading rumble and bellowing of cattle in all-out mad stampede.

The sky was lit up by the blazing buildings and the only man to notice that the train had pulled out and away from the siding was the private who had been ordered back to the fort to change out of his long johns.

He sat on the stoop of the sutler's store, sipping from a broken-necked bottle of brandy. Unable to find the key to the medicine cabinet, he had kicked in the door of the deserted store, busted the chain on the liquor cupboard and made his selection.

The fumes were rampant inside his skull by now and he took a long swig, gasped as the fiery liquid seared his throat and frowned as he watched the train snake out into the night, soon lost to sight.

'Hey! Yez're early! I — I'm s'posed to be one of the guards on that train t'morra! . . . Aaaah, hell with you. It's a borin' chore anyways . . . ' Another long swig; by now he could hardly see, or hold two consecutive thoughts for more than a few seconds. But: 'Hey! Why din' you blow the goddam' whistle?' he slurred half aloud. 'Aw, shoot! I like the sound of a train whistle.' He chuckled and cupped a hand around his mouth, throwing back his head, '*Whoooo-whooo-ooooooo . . .* '

He held his long drawn-out imitation of a train whistle until he ran out of breath, then flopped backwards, gasping. He rolled on to his side and was violently sick, after which he began to snore.

A patrol, eventually remembering the guns, found him that way, a quarter-hour later. But unhindered and undetected, the train thundered away into the prairie darkness.

# 2

## White Indian

He moved like a shadow and with as little sound.

He was wearing buckskin trousers and high moccasins, a buckskin pullover shirt, belted at the waist, and a faded red bandanna tied around his long black hair.

Clint Taggart was a white man but long ago he had decided that paleface clothing was more of a hindrance than a help when stalking game — or men — in brush country. The Indians had learned over hundreds of years not to wear loose-fitting clothes that could snag on twigs or rough bark, making only a small sound, but enough to warn any prey they were seeking. In their way of life missed prey meant, more often than not, an empty belly. Indians had taught him, too, that wild animals were sensitive to ground vibrations. So now, when he took a step forward, he did so carefully, adjusting his body weight, gently pressing the ball of his foot to the ground first, slightly bending the knee, moving the hips a little forward and bringing the other leg on directly in line with the first, then repeating the process. This way the body absorbed most vibrations before they could be transmitted through the ground and warn some hiding animal. And alerting this big cat he was stalking was the very last thing Taggart wanted to do.

He had been hunting it for two years now, following sightings all over the county, once crossing the high range itself, but always the mountain lion had outsmarted him.

Now he was closer than he had ever been before.

He moved forward through the young trees and green brush silently, no more than a deadly shade, clutching his flatbow with its sinew and bullsnake backing, arrow held firmly, razor-sharp point downwards, nock ready for fitting to the greased deer-tendon string. The bow was made of osage, the wood favoured by the Indians; he had seen no profit in an English-style longbow when this type of weapon had served the redman so well over the centuries.

It was important to him that he killed the big cat with this bow; it belonged to a special man, a Kiowa, Red Wing Swift, though his whiteman name was more mundane: Tommy Crow.

An old man with long, iron-grey hair hanging in plaits with charms and totems worked into the strands, Red Wing had made the bow himself, and the arrows, although Taggart had replaced the knapped flint points with his own design of razorsharp iron. He wanted that arrow to penetrate deeply once it found target.

'There is much spirit in this bow,' the old Indian had told him when presenting the weapon. 'Your arrows will fly true and it is right that they should kill the Big One.'

Now Taggart could smell rotting meat and he knew that it was the carcass of the newborn calf the cat had killed and snatched from the womb of the mother even during the birthing process. Then it had wantonly torn the udder from the suffering beast, left it to bleed to death, while he snapped the calf's neck with a single bite behind the head, and made off with the prize into the hills.

The same old pattern — almost as if the cat *knew*, and was taunting him to come after it. *Well, I'm coming this time* . . .

And there it was: big and tawny, grunting and snuffling into the calf's ribcage. It would be rotten meat by now, alive with maggots, but the cat likely preferred it that way.

*Enjoy it, you son of a bitch: it's the last thing you'll savour on this earth!*

He glided down a small slope until he was slightly below the ledge where the cat was eating; this was what he wanted.

16

He aimed to nail the lion in full flight, chest and belly exposed, making fine targets. Very risky, but he had decided it had to be this way. Only courage could hope to expunge the misery of the last two years without Lorene. If he found he lacked the wherewithal, then so be it, but he had to face the test he had set himself. Red Wing would approve.

Arrow pocked, two fingers under the fletching, one above, he drew back the string, feeling the seventy-pound pull knot his muscles: first his arms, then his shoulders and chest. The heel of his hand touched his cheekbone, anchoring just below his right eye, the string taut, the fibres stretched and compressed. Both his eyes were open, unblinking.

'Come on!' he yelled suddenly and almost immediately the cat was coming, launching itself off the ledge, jaws still dripping with gore and maggots, snarling, hate-filled yellow eyes finding him instantly. Stretched out, almost eight feet long, the cat hurtled towards him, gleaming fangs bared, claws unsheathed, ready and eager to tear him apart. Immobile, he opened his straining fingers. The string twanged and hurled the arrow with its specially made long metal tip straight at the cat at the start of its downward plunge towards Taggart.

Then came the sound he had been waiting for — aching to hear for two long, grieving years, ever since he had found the ravaged body of Lorene: the unmistakable high-pitched, rasping death-scream of the big cat.

Its body fell just short of where he stood, but momentum slammed it against his legs and knocked him over. The tawny body rolled on to his sprawling form and he instinctively snatched at his knife.

But there was no need; the arrow had penetrated the chest, all the way up to the turkey-feathers of the fletching; which meant there was thirty one and a half inches of laboriously worked dogwood shaft piercing the big cat's heart and other vital organs in the body cavity. Life would have left it in seconds.

Taggart lay there, his own heart hammering, but slowing now, content to feel the dead weight of the big cat across his lower body, its blood soaking through his buckskins.

'Now you can truly rest, Lorene,' he murmured to the bright blue cloudless sky he could see through the breeze-stirred branches above him. Exhausted, years of stress and tension finally draining from him, he closed his eyes and actually drifted into a half-sleep . . .

A man's voice woke him, and, with a start, he rolled swiftly, kicking free of the lion's heavy body, hand groping for the bow.

'God almighty! I thought he'd got you after all!'

Taggart strained his head around, recognizing Jimmy Morse's voice now, seeing the man in range clothes, carrying a rifle in one hand, silhouetted against the blazing sun.

'What're you doing up here?' he

asked, voice raspy, mouth dry, his body crying out for cool water.

Morse squatted down, a rangy man, in his late forties, rugged face sheened with sweat and smeared with trail dirt. 'Come lookin' for you.'

'You know better than that, Jimmy! This was something I had to do alone.'

'Sure. Wasn't gonna interfere unless that cat got the better of you. And, man! He's a beauty, ain't he?'

'He's dead, that's all I care. I'm still waiting for you to tell me why you came. You were supposed to be in town picking up that load of new tools from the freight depot.'

'Did that. Ran into a feller askin' all over town for you.'

Taggart stiffened and Morse gave him a hand to get completely out from under the dead lion now. He was taller than Morse, younger by nigh on ten years, wide-shouldered and long-legged, looking like some kind of Daniel Boone in his bloody buckskins and bandanna headband. Steel-grey eyes narrowed. 'He got a name, this man?'

Morse shook his head. 'I never heard it and he was careful not to mention it. Big feller, bigger'n you. In his fifties, with a face harder'n a granite outcrop.'

'How'd he carry his guns?'

Morse frowned. 'How'd you know he was totin' more than one gun? You been expectin' him, or someone like him, mebbe?'

Taggart shrugged. 'Description could fit a lot of men I've known. Two guns, you say? Crossed bullet belts, *buscadero* rig, tied down holsters, butts-forward for cross-draw . . . ?'

Morse smiled crookedly now. 'You do know him, don't you? Yeah, *buscadero* rig, gun-butts forward. One other thing: he smokes a pipe with a carved cherrywood bowl — seen it stickin' outta his shirt pocket.'

'That clinches it. His name's Buck Kirby. But damned if I know why he'd be looking for me.'

'One way to find out . . . '

Taggart paused. 'You go back, and if

he shows at the spread, keep him there. I'll be along.'

'What you gonna do now? Skin out that son of a bitch?' Jimmy Morse indicated the dead cat, joshing, but surprised when Taggart nodded, touching his knife.

'Yeah. Want to take the hide to a . . . place I know. I'll be in by sundown.'

Jimmy Morse nodded slowly. 'You sure picked up a lotta Injun ways. You're takin' it to her, ain't you?'

'Be in by sundown, Jimmy,' Taggart repeated and waited solemnly while Morse stood, nodded, and walked back over the ridge to where his mount was tethered.

When he had gone Clint Taggart unsheathed his hunting knife and stooped over the big cat, making the first cut in the tawny hide just beneath the arrow's entrance hole.

\* \* \*

It was Buck Kirby, all right. Taggart recognized him as he rode into the

22

ranch yard, aglow in crimson with an edge of gold as the sun balanced on the crest of the western range.

He rode the big sorrel up to the corral fence and Jimmy Morse strolled across from the bunkhouse where there was a lot of noise as the other ranch hands joshed each other just before supper. Morse held the reins as Taggart swung down, smelling the stench of the big cat on the bloodstained buckskins. He jerked his head towards the shadowed porch.

'That the feller you figured it was?'

'That's him.' Taggart slid his Winchester from the saddle scabbard. He was wearing a gunbelt and six-shooter now and stepped around Morse, indicating the horse. 'He's been three days with me in the brush, a lot of it ground-hitched. So if he wants to canter around some, put him in the empty corral.'

Strolling towards the porch, Taggart watched the big man there rise from the sagging old cane chair, step forward and lean on the rail. He took the cherrywood pipe from between his teeth and smoke puffed out of his mouth as he spoke. 'Still playin' Injun, I see.'

'Not playing, Buck. Dead serious about it.'

Kirby spat. 'Whatever you say. Still reckon you got some taint in your blood, way back.'

'Could be. Don't matter one way or another. What're you doing here? Still a sergeant?'

'Hell no. Captain now.'

'Must've settled your differences with Eadie.'

'He moved on — and upwards. I worked for this. How about you? Tired of ranchin' yet?'

'No.'

'Heard you had some . . . bad luck couple years back. Figured you might show at headquarters, ready to re-up.'

Taggart stepped up on to the porch, leaned his hips against the rail, still holding the rifle. 'Now, why would I do that?'

24

Buck Kirby smiled without humour, showing some large, stained teeth. 'You know what they say. 'Once a Ranger . . .''

' . . . Always a Ranger: Yeah I know, Buck. But the Rangers didn't want me. Leastways, they said it without saying it, if you know what I mean. I'm not sorry I quit.'

'Aw, hell, Clint, that was a long time ago. What . . . Eight, nine years back now. It's just the way things were then. Nothin' personal.'

Taggart stared at the man, then shook his head slowly. 'You ain't changed. Say what suits you at the moment.'

'Or what I'm ordered to.'

'Oh? Someone ordered you to lay it on the line for me like before? Quit, or be dishonourably discharged?' Taggart thrust off the rails. 'We'll have supper and talk later. Right now, I need to wash up.'

'Won't take long, what I want . . . ' began Kirby but Taggart was already going into the house, shutting the door behind him.

The Ranger's craggy face registered displeasure but then he dropped back into the cane chair and relit his pipe.

Well, he'd known it wouldn't be easy coming here — He was a man who hated to eat crow, no matter what the reason — specially if he was ordered to do it . . .

The Mexican cook, old Rico, had a tin hip-bath full of hot water and suds waiting on the back porch. 'You scrub all that . . . stuff offa you, boss,' he said, scratching his fat belly. 'It time you get rid of it for good. Jimmy tell me you got the jaguar. Things be better now.'

'*Gracias*, Rico.'

Taggart stripped and stepped into the bath, Rico taking the smelly buckskins outside. As he scrubbed and lay back, letting the suds lap all the way up under his jaw, Clint Taggart closed his eyes and he felt the muscles relaxing, the tension draining away.

*Two terrible years — And, how long*

*did Kirby say, before that? Eight —
nine . . . ?*

*Yeah — about nine years ago when
he crossed the Rio without Ranger
sanction and . . .*

* ★ ★ ★

Hell, there'd been no progress made at
all with the abduction of that railroad
owner's young daughter. She had been
snatched while riding with some young
buck approved by her mother and the
society she was a part of, and whoever
had taken her left her escort stone cold
and very dead in the middle of the
riding-path in quiet, shadowed woods.
'Breeding' didn't necessarily mean
courage.

The father, man named Linus
O'Keefe, raised merry hell and, being a
Texan, he insisted the Rangers be
brought into the case and to hell with
the US marshals.

'If anyone can find Bonnie, it's the
Rangers. If they can't . . . ' O'Keefe had

27

had to pause, swallow, and even then his voice trembled as he added: 'if they can't — well, Mother and I'll just have to accept that . . . she's . . . gone . . . '

There had been no ransom demands and Clint Taggart, a Ranger for five years at that time, had a strong hunch that Bonnie O'Keefe, with her fine, smooth skin and golden hair and blue eyes, was on her way down the white slave line.

It had endings in Mexico City and to the south, all the way into South America. And once the victim was on a sailing ship to that destination — well, no one but the depraved 'customers' would ever see her again.

'You can't know that, Clint,' Captain Eadie said when Taggart put forth his theory. 'Anyway, things are mighty touchy with Mexico — again! — right now, so we can't go making accusations or expect any co-operation.'

'It could be done without their co-operation, Captain,' Taggart pointed out quietly.

Eadie was appalled. 'My God! Get that out of your head right now, Taggart! Christ, man, they'd disband the Rangers and throw us all to the wolves! Now I don't want to hear another thing about it! Get back to your company, report to Sergeant Kirby and tell him you are hereby confined to barracks until further notice!'

Confined to barracks . . . While that young girl went through the torments of hell and had nothing to look forward to except more hell! No, sir!

By midnight that same day Taggart was across the Rio. His old mentor, Red Wing Swift, a Kiowa Indian who had somehow hovered in the background for most of his life, even before he joined the Rangers, was with him. They were afoot but within an hour Red Wing had horses and a loaded pack-mule for them. Taggart never asked how come, but later he saw the Indian cleaning his hunting-knife.

They both knew this country, having made many covert excursions here stealing horses and sometimes cattle from the huge Mexican *estancias* that were more like empires than privately owned *ranchos*, deeded down through generations from the time of the conquistadores.

From time to time their escapades had brushed white slavers, and inevitably each encounter had ended in a gunfight or a night attack by both of them, sometimes rescuing the girl or girls, sometimes not. But the slavers all finished up dead one way or another.

This time, it would be harder. Because there was such a hue and cry raised in Texas, the fires stoked by O'Keefe's money and power, it would drive the slavers deep underground. There was even the chance that, hounded, and with the law closing in, the slavers might kill the hostage and Bonnie O'Keefe would never be found.

Taggart wondered where he would find the guts to go back and report *that* to Linus O'Keefe.

But they were here and there was no

time to waste. They made contact with men they had known from the raiding days, and all were reluctant, if not downright fearful, at passing on any news that would help. In fact, four men were sent to find the gringos and kill them. It had been Red Wing who had heard them first and they set up their camp so that the killers would think they were seeing their quarry in their sleeping-bags.

As they stepped confidently into the faint light of the dying camp-fire, the Kiowa's hunting bow twanged! and a Mexican screamed as a flint-tipped arrow pierced him through the throat. Taggart's rifle thundered and rent the night, bullets finding their targets. Two of the three slavers went down, dead before they hit the ground. The third was shot through the left hip — deliberately — and fell writhing and screaming.

The Kiowa squatted beside him, knife in one hand, a glowing, sharpened stick in the other, and he said quietly in

Spanish, 'We will talk now, *señor* . . . '

The man did a lot more screaming. But he talked and gave them the lead they needed before he died. It meant a long, fast ride to the south, all the way to Monterrey. From there, the trail would lead west, towards the Gulf coast at Matamoros.

The Kiowa had kept quiet about the bullet that had torn across his lower ribs during the brief gunfight.

'Judas, Red Wing, you damn' old fool! This should've had treatment a couple of days ago!'

'I will live — and so will you, if you ride with the Wind Spirit. I will ask him to guide you and speed you on your way.' The old man winked. 'Or maybe just cross my fingers for good luck. Maybe both, and then we will be winners — white and red working together for once.'

Taggart grinned, always amused when the Kiowa made light of his beliefs and their great relationship.

So Taggart took both horses and rode

with the wind. It took him four days and when he reached Matamoros the southbound schooner was already anchored offshore. Discreet enquiries, and more than a little silver, helped him find out that the Golden One, as the O'Keefe girl had been named, was being held in a small shack amongst the dunes just south of town.

Taggart took the sawn-off shotgun from the leather boot attached to his saddle, loaded it, put spare shells in his pockets, and waited until dark.

The abductors were confident they were safe. There was a man in the shadows near the door, seated, and dozing in a chair. Soon after Taggart spotted him there was no chance he would ever awaken. But the chair was old and weak, and gave way with a loud, splintering crack of ancient timber.

The murmuring in the shack ceased instantly and an American voice called softly, 'Gus? You better not be boozin' again, feller! *Gus*!'

They were professionals and the man figured he had said enough, fell silent. Crouched in the brush beside the dead man, Taggart held the shotgun ready, hammers cocked, and waited. He heard a door open at the rear, leather hinges dried out and creaking. At the same time the front door opened; the lamp inside had already been extinguished.

Taggart had earlier looked in through the single window, the glass was smudged and did not give him a very clear picture of the set-up inside. But he had seen enough, knew that the bunk where they had the girl bound and gagged was along the left-hand wall, towards the rear. There was a table and he had counted three shadows.

Now he saw one of those shadows, snaking belly-down across the stoop, black against black. He even smelled the hot oil from the lamp, he was that close. So, one out the back, one at the front — where was the third?

He had no time to think about it. The one from the back had ghosted down the side of the shack, spotted his location, and shot at him. It was hasty but the bullet still slammed into Taggart's side, lurching him out of cover. The man at the front, instead of shooting, tried to leap to his feet so as to make a better shot. He never made it.

Clint Taggart's shotgun roared and the buckshot shredded the man's belly. He died screaming as Taggart, down on one knee now, whirled and triggered at the man at the side of the building. Splinters flew but the heavy balls tore through the seawind-scoured wood and blew away half the killer's chest.

Before the man went down, Taggart was moving forward, slowed some by the wound, but gritting his teeth and going in at a crouch, with six-gun in hand. He dived through the doorway and, as he had hoped, the one still inside fired, startled. His gunflash showed him clearly, crouched at this end of the bunk. Taggart twisted in midair, the pain wrenching a grunt from him. Then he was sliding across the floor, Colt held in front of him, thumbing the hammer, trigger depressed. Three bullets hurled the slaver against the wall and he fell, sobbing, boot-heels drumming briefly.

Taggart lay there, huddled, feeling the blood and pain in his side. He tore off his neckerchief and wadded it over the wound.

'It's OK, Bonnie. I'm a Texas Ranger, and I'll take you back home . . . '

*I'm a Texas Ranger* . . . He should never have said it. People from the town and nearby fishermen's shacks had come running and some of them had heard.

A Ranger had no jurisdiction south of the Rio, didn't even have official sanction to be there.

Clint Taggart knew he would not be returning to a hero's welcome.

# 3

## Out Of The Past

Supper was over and Kirby and Taggart sat on the stoop of the front porch, both smoking in the cool evening.

'You sure stirred up a hornet's nest, Clint, comin' back with that gal. You were lucky they didn't toss you in the stockade and throw away the key.'

Taggart smiled thinly. 'Bonnie put in a word for me with Daddy.'

Kirby saw no humour in it and Taggart heard it in the man's voice. 'Pure goddamn luck! By God, I even wished I'd been the one to break orders and cross the Rio . . . '

'I'll bet you did, Buck. You were always an envious sonuver.'

He felt Kirby stiffen. 'Let's not get back to namecallin'!'

'No. There was too much of that

when I brought in the girl. Until O'Keefe shouldered his way in and called in favours owed him by state senators and so on who wouldn't've been in office if they hadn't had his money backing them at election time.'

'Must've been the best thing ever happened to you!' The tight-lipped envy was still showing in the man's tone.

'Best thing that ever happened to me was Lorene,' Taggart told him quietly. 'And O'Keefe made that happen for me.'

The railroad man hadn't minced words when he had fronted the Rangers and other lawmen who wanted to jail Taggart for causing such political tension with Mexico.

'This man saved my daughter and I want him rewarded.'

'Rewarded!' Captain Eadie leapt to his feet, fist slamming down on his desk. 'Good God, man! He disobeyed standing orders! Killed Mexican nationals, had no authorization whatsoever!'

'His instincts, raw courage and

initiative were all he needed, Captain, and my daughter wouldn't be here now if it wasn't for Ranger Taggart. I intend to reward him and I will bring pressure to bear so that no charges will be laid against him. I can do it, Captain! And I will!'

Eadie knew the railroad man spoke the truth. Grumpily, actually admitting defeat, he said, 'No Ranger can accept bounty or reward whilst in the Service, sir!'

O'Keefe turned to the silent Taggart. 'Clint, they're right, but you must see you have no future here now. I may be able to make them drop the charges, but how long will you be able to stay in the Rangers? They'll make life hell for you until you resign. Why not accept that as a fact? Quit the Rangers now and there's nothing to stop you from accepting the ten thousand dollars I intend to reward you with — more if you wish. To me, my daughter's life can not have a price put upon it.'

There were indrawn breaths and then

sudden silence. At last Taggart cleared his throat.

'Mr O'Keefe, I only did the job I felt I was supposed to. I can't accept that money.'

That brought even more stunned looks. O'Keefe smiled slowly; a short, slim man, dressed immaculately, with a lined face. The smile seemed to smoothe out some of those lines.

'Bonnie said you would refuse. But you have no say in it, Clint. I want to reward you and I will. If, somehow, you stay on, eventually you'll leave the Rangers or retire, and that money will still be waiting for you.' He shook a finger lightly at the stunned Ranger. 'I'm a man used to having my own way, sir.'

As it happened, Taggart didn't have to wait long to collect the reward.

The Rangers made it clear he would have to quit or face charges that would put him behind bars for a long time. They didn't want this because the publicity wouldn't do the Service any good and already it was hard to find men qualified to do the tough job required of a Texas Ranger.

Besides, he and Lorene, young and madly in love, wanted to get married and the sooner the better. With $10,000 — a sum which took their breaths away — they could find the ranch they both wanted and develop it, make a fine, rewarding life together, with their children.

So he had quit the Rangers, married Lorene, and settled on this ranch north of San Antonio, in the shadow of the Balcones escarpment and the Edwards plateau.

They had only one child, a little girl, named Rachel, after Taggart's mother. It had been a difficult birth, resulting in Lorene being unable to bear any more children.

Devastating as the news was, their marriage never flagged and the child spent her first six years at the ranch, until the day when, in the forest above San Felipe Canyon, the big mountain lion had caught her on a ledge and leapt at the small, cowering figure.

But Lorene had seen the danger, threw herself between the big cat and the child . . .

★ ★ ★

'Hey! Are you listening?'

Taggart snapped his head up, aware that his cigarette had burned down too low to draw on now without scorching his lips. He crushed it against the weathered stoop and turned to Buck Kirby.

'What were you saying, Buck?'

'Hell! I ain't going through it all again. Boils down to this.' He paused, toyed with his cold pipe a few moments, then said with a rush, 'They want you back in the Rangers.'

Taggart went very still, straining to see Kirby's face in the dim light. So this was why he had wanted to come talk out here in the dark . . .

Clint felt mild amusement at the

knowledge of Kirby's discomfort. 'You travelled all this way to ask me that?'

'Well? Yes or no?'

Taggart shrugged. 'I'm happy enough here, Buck.'

'Yeah, you say. But I've heard about what happened to your wife and I'm real sorry about that, Clint. I liked Lorene. Kid OK now?'

'Away at school.'

Kirby waited for more information but it was not forthcoming. He sighed, took a deep breath. 'Clint, you hear about that big theft of guns about six months ago? From Arlington Armory up near Fort Worth?'

Taggart nodded. 'Everyone heard about it. They practically burned down the town, didn't they?'

'Yeah. Ruthless sons of bitches. Stole the goddamn train! Offloaded the guns in the middle of nowhere, stoked up the loco and set it runnin' loose along a single track! Judas, it was lucky it ran outta steam — literally! — just before that big bridge over Mesquite Creek

Gorge. Passenger train was headin' towards it, nowhere to go, looked like one helluva massacre about to happen — but the loco trundled to a stop, right in the middle of the bridge.'

'Never heard that part before. Where'd they unload the guns?'

'Place don't matter. Thing is they disappeared. Nigh on a thousand brand-new Sharps, fallin'-block, case-extractors and all.'

'Worth a lot of money — and one hell of a haul to just . . . disappear.'

'Ain't the worst part. Car-load of ammunition, close to a million rounds, was with 'em.'

The old Ranger instincts began to stir. 'Sounds like someone was getting ready to start a war.'

Kirby lit his pipe, eyes swivelled towards Taggart.

'They were.'

'Were . . . ?'

'Uh-huh. Guns were bound for Louisiana. Some loco French count was financin' a revolution, claimed his

44

ancestors founded the state and he was the rightful ruler. All crazy stuff. Anyway, he had some kinda fit and died and the guns were left, abandoned — or hidden damn well.' He paused. 'I tell you, Louisiana is one place we never thought of lookin'.'

'You'd wonder why someone would let all that money just lie around. The men who stole them in the first place were likely just gun-runners, had no interest in any crazy revolution as long as they got paid . . . '

'Right. But, bein' gun-runners, they were always lookin' for places to . . . well, run guns.'

'Oh-oh! I think I see — '

Kirby continued quickly, not wanting Taggart to spoil his spiel. 'Yeah. Someone knew where they were — and that someone made himself a deal to deliver them guns to a group who would pay off big.'

Taggart frowned. 'Repeaters would be more in demand, wouldn't they?'

'Sure. But how many repeating rifles

you heard about being stole in quantities like them Sharps? We make it damn hard so the gun-runners have to peddle whatever they can get. The older the gun, the better, far as we're concerned.'

'And who's got this lot?'

'I'll come to that. Thing is, we came in late on the deal. They'd already moved 'em. By ship across the Gulf, aimin' to unload on the Mexican coast and then take 'em cross-country.'

'Sounds like a good enough plan.'

'Sure. But we got on to it and alerted the Mexicans. Somehow word got out that they'd be walkin' into a trap if they tried to land the guns in Mexico, so they put into Padre Island on the Texas coast, south of Kingsville.' He looked and sounded mildly embarrassed. 'Caught us with our pants down. But thing is, we know they're movin' 'em overland, now. But only some. Seems one of them Gulf storms hit Padre Island hard, like they usually do. Destroyed or washed away into deep water a lot of the guns and ammo. We know of only two wagonloads now, and we think we have a line on where they're going.' He paused again, looking intently at Taggart now. 'The only way they *can* go is run for the border, and cross somewhere between Brownsville and Rio Bravo.'

Taggart remained silent, forcing Kirby to continue.

'We figure they'll either make for Matamoros and try to pick up another ship there, or head down to Monterrey — through that country where you tracked around until you found Bonnie O'Keefe.'

Taggart almost smiled as he said, 'All unofficially, without Ranger sanction as I recall.'

Kirby's indrawn breath was a long, deep one.

'Yeah. Well, we know what happened because of that. Thing is, we don't have anyone who knows that area, but this is so important, we've got a sort of unspoken say-so from the Texas senate to send some men down there, across the Rio, and head off them guns. Officially, they'll deny any such sanction was ever discussed, let alone given, of course . . . '

'Of course,' Taggart said mock seriously, a strange quirky humour stirred by Kirby's words.

The Ranger said stiffly, 'Hell, they're US Army ordnance, after all! We're within our rights to try and recover 'em!'

'You damn hypocrite,' Taggart said, chuckling. 'Man, this must've cost you plenty to come down here and ask me to guide your team so they can intercept those guns!'

Kirby remained silent for a long minute, then he asked, hoarsely, 'Well? You gonna do it?'

★ ★ ★

Jimmy Morse tightened the tie-thongs on the packs astride the wooden frame and looked across the back of the docile packhorse at Taggart.

48

'Never figured you'd ever do them Rangers a favour, Clint. Not after the way they treated you.'

There was quiet criticism in his voice. Taggart was going to ignore it, but Morse was an old friend as well as a mighty good ramrod and he owed him some sort of explanation.

'Doing myself the favour, way I figure it, Jimmy.'

'How, for Pete's sake? Puttin' your life on the line for men who treated you like dirt, prodded by envy and plain jealous because O'Keefe paid you that reward?' Morse shook his head slowly. 'Man, you are somethin', Clint!'

Taggart tucked the end of the cinchstrap through the brass ring on his saddle, yanked it tight and patted the big sorrel lightly. 'I need this chore, Jimmy.'

Morse frowned and, after a moment nodded. 'Yeah. Should've seen it. You've had it hard in the coupla years since Lorene got mauled by that cougar. Now you've finally nailed the son of a bitch, laid that part to rest. Yeah, be best you get away from here for a spell. But it don't make it any the less dangerous.'

'All that kept me going at times was hating that big cat. I need something else now, something different, to shake the remnants from me. I was kinda crazy for a long time, I guess, but . . . '

He paused and Morse nodded, not speaking not trying to force any more words of explanation from Taggart. He knew how Lorene's death had torn the man apart, especially the way she had died, under the fangs and claws of that cougar. And her sacrificing herself for the child, Rachel, that way.

Jimmy Morse had never been married but he somehow savvied how a mother could do that kind of thing without thought for her own safety.

The love between Taggart and Lorene had been as powerful as he had ever seen in his forty-something years. He had been mildly surprised at the time that Taggart hadn't contemplated suicide, as he had seen happen to other men so strongly attached to their women. But that wasn't Clint Taggart. And the wise old Kiowa had given him some sense of purpose by encouraging him to hunt down that killer cat.

Apart from spending two years of his life searching for the mountain lion, Clint knew Rachel would need him. He had tried hiring a governess but wasn't satisfied, and this last year the child had been away at some fancy 'School for Young Ladies' in Denver, Colorado, at the suggestion of Lorene's mother, who lived in nearby Aurora where Rachel could spend weekends and short breaks from schooling. For the longer holidays she would come here to the L Slash C ranch.

With most of his cash tied up in land and cattle and a dam he had built so as to ensure year-round water, it must have been one hell of a strain, running this ranch. It had to pay its way, so he could meet the heavy fees of the school and regular, unavoidable ranch costs. Then he had needed funds and time to chase down news about that murderous mountain lion. Taggart had travelled hundreds of miles checking sightings, most of which were useless, motivated by someone hoping to claim the $500 reward he had posted for a definite lead.

And, in the midst of it, the old Kiowa, Tommy Crow, had died. Simply announced one day that it was his time, the Great Spirit had called him and he would go into the wilderness, find a suitable cave and wait for his passing.

Sounded all loco to Jimmy, although he allowed that Indians had strange ways and no white man could deter them once they decided it was time to join their ancestors.

Before he went, Tommy Crow — Red Wing Swift, as Taggart preferred to call him — had made that bow, the 'Cat-Killer' — the one that would avenge Lorene's death.

Morse was kind of irritated at the calm way Taggart accepted all this, but then the man had lived with Indians for years. While he had still been in the late stages of early childhood, his father had been killed by Comanches. Red Wing, riding with the war party, had somehow felt an attachment to the boy and taken him into his tepee, the Indian's way of saying he would rear the boy as his own son. Comanche and Kiowa raiding parties quite often took promising young white males back to join the tribe. When it came time to return to the white man's world, Red Wing had accompanied Clint, stayed, and been no less than a watchdog, remaining close even during Taggart's adult life, including the time he had been in the Rangers.

There had always been a powerful bond between them, and when the old Kiowa had died within days of giving the bow to Taggart, Clint had somehow known without even leaving the ranch that Red Wing Swift's spirit had flown from this world.

All this must have been a strain but Clint had been strong enough to carry it, bore it silently, holding it in. Now it was time for a complete change, to clear his system of all that negative hatred, to find a new, more rewarding kind of life.

'You're doin' it the hard way, Clint,' Morse said, without having to go into detail; he knew Taggart savvied what he was saying.

'Don't know no other way when you get right down to it, Jimmy.' He swung aboard the sorrel, adjusted his hat and looked down at Morse. 'You'll manage OK. If I'm not back by, say, mid-August, you start the trail drive. Just watch that buyer from St Louis; he's always first on the spot at the railhead, but he's tight with a dollar.'

Morse grinned. 'I've watched you handle him often enough. Reckon I can get top dollar.'

They shook hands briefly and, before Taggart touched his spurs to the sorrel, Morse said, 'You keep that bow?'

Taggart shook his head. 'Rightfully belonged to Red Wing,' and the ramrod knew that Taggart had taken the bow to the Kiowa's cave and laid it alongside the old man's body, which would be already starting to mummify in the dry winds.

Just as he had taken the hide of the cougar to the special glade where Lorene's grave was, and stretched it over the mound, likely pegging it down, a symbol of the ending of the long hunt.

Taggart might not have any Indian blood in his veins, but he sure had absorbed plenty of their ways in his years with those Kiowas.

# 4

## Contrabandistas

The big, white-painted hacienda sprawled over the slopes of the hill on the south side of the San Antonio River. It offered fine views from almost every window and patio archway, caught the cool breezes from the river, which blew across from the Anglo settlement on the north side; they had cattle-pens and vegetable-markets over there, as if planned to waft bad smells into the Hispanic section.

There had been much blood spilled here during the Texas Revolution in the late 1820s and some men, Anglo and Spanish, had long memories, determined never to forget the conflict and ancestors who had met their deaths at that time.

Don Diego Escalante was such a

man: small, rawboned with a long face and gimlet-eyed. The hacienda belonged to him and he ran it like a feudal lord, a law unto himself. Beyond the fine white walls, topped with kiln-fired clay tiles so as to shed rainwater on to the gardens inside the compound, United States law might apply — in fact, was meant to apply inside, too, but Don Diego and his underlings chose to ignore this. He was the master, the law-giver, the enforcer. He treated his workers harshly. There were whippings, military-style torture, such as tying a *peon* to a wagon wheel and leaving him there for two, three days, or longer, without food or water; then, perhaps, the unfortunate would still have to face the lash.

Don Diego lived his own life on his own terms and had sufficient wealth and power to maintain this without undue interference from the Anglos. Occasionally, so as to scotch any unflattering rumours about the *estancia* and the goings-on there, he allowed visitors, carefully screened first, naturally.

They saw men and women working the estate, while a strolling trio of musicians, guitar, flute and a woman singer with a sweet voice, played music of *Old Mejico*. The visitors were impressed, if not astonished, and were wined and dined within the high-ceilinged great hall with its stained-glass windows and swinging candelabras made of iron forged in old Castille, gently lighting a few original Old Masters paintings from Spain and Holland and France. They always went away more than satisfied with the way Don Diego *appeared* to run his domain.

Immensely wealthy, Escalante kept track of politics in Mexico, south of the Rio. He dared not go there in person for his name was on a very secret list kept in the Citadel in Mexico City. This was a list of enemies of the state, a death list. Once, Don Diego's personal guards had caught three assassins who, under torture, claimed to have been sent by *El Presidente* himself. Don Diego smiled in understanding: it was good to know he was still feared in the highest places — and rightly so. He would have been feared even more if something hadn't gone so terribly wrong with that arms theft, half a year ago, when his men had virtually razed Fort Worth to smoking ashes. *Madre de Dios! Desastre!*

If only he had not allied himself with that lunatic Frenchman who wanted only to indulge a stupid fantasy about reclaiming and ruling Louisiana, already naming himself King Marius the First, carrying a jewelled crown everywhere with him. The man had employed idiots who had not only lost him Louisiana, but more than half the guns, before Don Diego had a chance to pull his own meticulously planned double-cross.

Escalante had intended those guns for allies in Mexico, men who, at a word from him, would make a concerted move on several strategic points in the north of the country, taking control of the military posts. Discipline was lax at such places, the *comandantes* grown lazy and fat and debauched, using their power for their own gratification, far from the eyes of Mexico City.

With all those weapons and the huge quantity of ammunition, he could have made his coup to take over northern Mexico, 'arranged' a deal with the *Estado Unidos* that would give him adequate protection, and see himself installed as *El Presidente* of a new Northern Province, a buffer state, independent of Mexico. (He considered this even less of a fantasy than King Marius's conquest of Louisiana.)

And beyond that, even, lay his true goal: the eventual reclamation of the southern part of the Republic of Texas, making it a Spanish possession once more, as it had been centuries earlier. One day it would happen! Back in Spain, there were allies who would back such a cause. It would take time, lots of time — but he had children who would carry on the fight if he died before its realization. Ah, yes — the children!

Here was the only sad note: a daughter, Consuela, fiery and passionate as any zealot but — inevitably and permanently a *femenino*. And then there was his only son, Franco. *El Torpe* — the Awkward One, or, as the Anglos say it, the Fumbler. It hurt to even think the boy's nick-name but, unfortunately, it was deserved. Twenty years old, the boy was two years his sister's senior, but he was as clumsy as a backward child. He forged ahead with schemes barely half-thought-through, eager, desperate to impress his father, leaving chaos and failure in his wake — every enterprise only serving to enhance his already tainted reputation. If only the boy would think, before he acted! He was brave enough — vicious enough, perhaps — not to let anything stand in his way, but . . . something was lacking. Ah! What a thrill it would be to have him succeed — just once!

Franco had begged and begged to be allowed to take charge of the gun wagons now ready to move south across the Rio, bound for Monterrey. Don Diego was tempted, but already there had been one disaster, with the ship being driven aground on Padre Island. Could he risk another by putting Franco in charge? Perhaps triggering a calamity of even greater magnitude . . . ?

*Dios*! It would be a tremendously big risk, giving Franco such responsibility . . . But if he were to pull it off! Ah, what it would do for the boy's esteem! What it would do for The Plan! And the fame of the Escalante family.

Just the thought made him catch his breath — but why not? Everything was prepared now, down to the last detail: border patrols bribed, *bandidos* paid not to attack the wagons, certain military officers given guarantees of a life of pleasure in the *Estados Unidos* — all Franco would have to do was follow the plan. He could do that! *Sí*! He had proved time and again that he could follow explicit orders, albeit as long as they were simplified. Anyway, there was alwaya Dolfo to stand by and guide him, see that everything was done according to instructions . . . and act as the boy's protector.

Hand trembling, he reached for the wine carafe, splashed some deep-red liquid into a gold-rimmed crystal glass and gulped it down. It was a measure of his agitation that he drank this way; normally he sipped and savoured such fine wine. He was breathing a little faster, now, his heart was beginning to race. He poured another glass, forced himself to sip this time, then, decisively, he tugged the gilt-and-red bell-rope beside the deep-purple velvet drapes. Almost immediately a uniformed servant appeared, holding open one half of the intricately carved oak door.

'At your service, *señor* . . . ?'

After clearing his throat Don Diego said in a hoarse whisper, 'Fetch Don Franco and Señor Dolfo — *con urgencia*.'

The Rangers took ten men with them, making an even dozen in the group.

Big Buck Kirby was tense — no one would use 'nervous' to describe such a man with the huge reputation he had built up — as Taggart led the way along the old well-remembered trail down to the Rio.

'We checked as well as we could, trying not to raise suspicions,' Kirby told Taggart quietly, easing his mount alongside. 'The Mexes have armed patrols of up to twenty men riding along this stretch, at random times.'

'Bigger deal than when Red Wing led me down here.'

'Times have changed, Clint. The politicians are at each others' throats over wetbacks. Everyone, including the Rangers, turns a blind eye to a few coming over, but they've been swarming across lately, and they're not all lookin' for work and what to them is high pay.'

Clint Taggart frowned. 'What're you saying?'

'*Bandidos*. Sons of bitches have realized it's an easy way to cross the border, join a bunch of genuine wetbacks, and then they hit the isolated spreads, clean 'em out of cattle and anything valuable, leave as many dead as it takes, then run back across the Rio. Fooled us for a time — we thought it was renegade Apaches, but it's *bandidos* all right.'

He went on to tell how pressure from the United States had eventually forced the Mexican government to make at least a token increase in their border patrols.

'Now it's working against us,' Taggart allowed. 'Well, we could hole up here for a spell, until the next patrol passes by. We'll cross right behind 'em, well before another lot are due.'

'Hope you're right,' Kirby said gruffly, obviously not pleased at having to put himself and his men in Taggart's hands. 'I haven't heard about them pullin' a fast one by sending a second patrol right after the first, yet, but — '

'Always the chance,' Taggart admitted. 'Yeah, but no one said this was going to be risk-free, Buck.'

Kirby drew down a deep breath. 'You're right.' He stood in the stirrups and turned to where his men were crowding around now. 'Hunt up some cover — we're gonna be here for a spell.'

A ripple of murmuring told him the men were already griping, none being particularly keen to venture south of the border in these unsettled times. But training took over and they scattered amongst the chaparral and small dry washes between the arid hills.

'How long, Cap?' one man called.

'I'll tell you when.'

'Or Taggart will!' someone called, voice a mite rough.

Clint smiled to himself; somehow, the Rangers were blaming him for this mission and all the risks it entailed. Just like the army: soldiers were always happier if they could find someone else to blame for any predicament they found themselves in. That was OK: it didn't bother him.

Of course, it wasn't made any easier by Buck Kirby's method of calling for 'volunteers'. He had merely walked along the assembled line, pointing to every second man, saying, 'You've volunteered — so have you — and you . . . '

Accordingly, they were a mixed bunch, veterans and men yet to gain experience in such operations. Only one or two of the latter, Rangers who, Kirby figured, could benefit from the clandestine mission. But Taggart could feel the tension that rode with them all and he figured many of the group would gladly have stayed behind in Texas, despite the danger money being offered — for those who survived.

⋆ ⋆ ⋆

They had been hiding for almost an hour when they heard the jingling of guthook spur rowels and riding gear, before they actually saw the ghostly Mexican patrol. A man in a drab uniform and wearing a peaked cap rode at the head of the group. Clint Taggart could see the sword at the man's belt, so there was no doubt this was the officer in charge. The soldiers followed in silence except for their riding-gear, which no one seemed to have thought of rendering quiet.

Taggart counted swiftly. Six lines, two abreast: a smaller patrol than he had been told to expect . . . *Oh-oh*. Could they have split up? The Rangers waited, gave it a few more minutes, and then Buck Kirby, wanting to make it plain that he was in charge no matter what authority Taggart had been given, said quietly, 'Move across. Now!'

'Damn it, Buck! Wait up!' hissed Taggart, but it was too late: the Rangers were already coming out of the chaparral, putting their mounts into the river's shallows. In minutes the leaders were half-way across, horses splashing.

Taggart stood in his stirrups, a hunch holding him back, straining to see to his right, the direction the patrol had come from. Nothing appeared to move in the deep darkness and he started to release the breath he had been holding. Seemed as if it was safe to make a move, anyway. At least there were no more riders suddenly appearing out of the night. But the Rangers were trying to cross as quickly as they could, not taking enough care to keep their passage silent. The mounts, like most horses, were not happy making a river crossing in the dark; they pranced and snorted, a couple balking. One whickered, not loudly, but . . .

The Mexican officer was no fool; apparently, he had heard something, had ridden to the rear as his men moved on, and checked the section of river they had just passed. Even if he couldn't make out the Rangers crossing in fans of spray that glinted silver in the starlight, he surely heard the splashing, maybe even that horse's whinny, or the half-smothered curses of the *norteam-ericanos*.

Wait! By God! He had stopped the patrol! It occurred suddenly to Taggart that maybe this particular patrol had been bribed to steer clear of a certain part of the river at a certain time. Then the officer suddenly yelled: 'Gringos!'

Taggart heard the man's sword rasp out of the scabbard, caught a glimpse of the slightly curved blade as it was lifted high. Then the officer was screaming in rapid-fire Spanish.

He never got to complete his orders. Some trigger-happy Ranger, tagging along behind the others in the river, opened up with his Winchester, unable to control his instincts at the alarm, levering and shooting, almost emptying the magazine. It spooked some of the others, the younger ones whose nerves had been stretched taut during the long wait on the Texas bank. Guns hammered, bullets slashing through the bunched Mexicans, hurling them out of their saddles. Wild Spanish curses and cries of agony and panic filled the dark. The river churned with prancing, rearing or racing mounts. American oaths mixed with roared commands. The men met, some tumbling into the muddy waters, one catching a boot in a stirrup and being dragged behind the panicking horse; if a bullet hadn't done for him, he must have drowned. Clint Taggart had his six-gun in hand and was working the sorrel through the shallows, triggering. Suddenly he found himself face to face with the Mexican officer. Blood gleamed on the dark face and teeth were bared as the sword-blade slashed at Clint's head. He flung up an arm. Sparks flew as the blade struck the Colt barrel, almost jarring the weapon from Taggart's grip. He fired and rolled sideways, felt the bite of the blade on his upper arm as the officer left the saddle, flailing awkwardly, and disappeared beneath the river's roiling surface.

A gun fired so close to his head that he felt the muzzle-flash scorch his ear and neck on that side. Head ringing, he swung the Colt around and up, triggered, thumbed the hammer again — but it clicked on an empty chamber. As a Mexican reeled out of his saddle, Taggart rammed the Colt back into his holster, slid his rifle from the scabbard.

The man he had just shot lunged upwards out of the water and he glimpsed a youngish, mad face, a small moustache beneath an aristocratic nose, and eyes insane with a lust to kill. A knife flashed in the man's hand. Taggart groaned as he felt the blade bite into his thigh and he swung the rifle down. The barrel was inches from the wild man's face when he fired the weapon one-handed. The Mexican was blown back a yard and disappeared under the surface.

As he wrenched the knife from his leg, Clint thought there seemed to be more Mexicans than there ought to be. Bunched riders were angling towards the American side of the river and the cries in Spanish hurled through the night reached his still-ringing ears so that he thought he must be translating wrongly.

'*Americanos*! The *guardabosques*! We have been betrayed! Run with the wagons!'

*The wagons*! Taggart stiffened, holding his quivering sorrel back as it made to plunge on. They had been recognized as Rangers. And there were the wagons, ahead, downstream, making their crossing at this very moment.

'It's a fake patrol!' Taggart yelled, his words heard easily now that the shooting was dying away. 'They were the gun-runners, dressed up! They're making the crossing now! Close in! Close in!'

His words stunned those Rangers still in their saddles and others among the wounded or dead cluttering this stretch of river. He spurred the sorrel down the middle of the shallows, throwing the Winchester to his shoulder. He could barely make out movement ahead, but through the noises in his head he heard the groaning of wagon wheels and a lot of shouting, mostly in Spanish. There were a couple of American voices, too, but they weren't Rangers — not that far ahead and coming from the Mexican side of the river.

Buck Kirby roused the remainder of his men, overcoming his shock at Taggart's words, knowing this was no time to doubt them or fuss about who was in charge.

By pure accident they had chosen to cross near the place used by the gun-runners, and had caught them flat-footed. Every second counted now or the tables would be turned.

Guns hammered from ahead, shotguns mixed with rifles and pistols. There was a lot of movement, the whiteness of churned water foaming around the wheels of the wagons as the *contrabandistas* whipped at the straining teams, got ropes on the wagons and used their mounts to lend their weight to the vehicles' progress, ropes drawn iron-bar taut.

More men were in the wagons, taking cover behind the wooden sides, shooting at the horsemen charging in, fanned out. At Buck Kirby's command, they formed the sickle-shaped charge made famous by the early Ranger troops, the one that put the fear of God — or the Devil, depending upon a man's beliefs — into the enemy. Legend had it that once the charge was started there was no escape. Men could either die or surrender and hope for mercy that wasn't always forthcoming, or, as had happened on a couple of occasions, the Rangers themselves could be killed — to a man.

But there was no stopping the charge.

Some of the gun-runners threw up their arms, having disposed of their weapons. One Mexican, tall in the saddle, shot two of them in wild rage at their capitulation. He roared at the others to fight to the death.

But it fell on deaf ears. Bullets slashed and cut down wagon-team horses and any man who moved, whether he held a gun or not. Bodies jammed against the half-submerged wheels or hung over the sides, a couple falling down into the traces with the surviving horses plunging dangerously close. The tall Mexican looked around him frantically, one arm hanging limply, blood dripping from pain-curled fingers. He lifted his gun in his other hand and fired at a Ranger, his bullet knocking the man out of the saddle. The tall one's horse was wounded and started to stumble. He jumped free, caught at the bridle of the downed Ranger's mount, and swung awkwardly into the saddle. The Ranger floundered and strained to bring up a dripping pistol. The tall man kicked him under the jaw, emptied his gun, rammed his mount into a startled *Anglo* rider and spurred around the back of one of the tilted, bogged wagons. All was lost! Only escape remained now.

Urging the straining mount behind a bogged, tilting wagon, he managed to reach the bank on the Mexican side. Gasping, his arm exploding with pain, he looked down at a body huddled at the edge on the bloodstained sand.

Just then, the crescent moon edged out from behind a cloud and washed its silver light over the scene of continuing massacre.

The tall one groaned aloud as he stared at those bullet-shattered features, feeling a strange rush through his body as if all his insides had fallen out.

Even in this half-light, made dimmer by the drifting gunsmoke, he recognized the man he was supposed to protect with his life — young Don Franco Escalante.

# 5

## Bring Me His Head!

It was mid-morning and the Ranger detachment looked mighty ragged. Six men had been wounded in the battle at the river last night, including Kirby and Taggart; two men had died, one the young rookie who had started the shooting.

'Didn't learn fast enough,' Kirby said, but although he was known as a hard man, Taggart didn't believe he was as unfeeling as he tried to make out. He seemed happier now the raid had been a success but was still a little reserved with Clint. 'Leastways, we got the guns back — and some prisoners.'

They were in the infirmary of the Ranger station in Laredo, where the doctor was cleaning up their wounds. He had stitched the gash in Taggart's thigh, told Clint he was lucky the knife had barely missed the big femoral artery.

'Takes a matter of seconds to hose out the body's blood once that artery's severed,' the medic added. 'You keep that pad and bandage on for at least a week — and no riding for a few days after that. Have a doctor take it off. Don't try to remove it yourself or you may break the stitching and start pumping your blood all over the place.'

'I remember you from before, as always being of great comfort when a man was wounded, or dying, Doc,' Clint told the half-smiling medic sourly.

Kirby had his wounds treated and bandaged and they went outside, sat down in the shade of the small *galeria* that looked out over the approaches to the station's main building. There was a Civil War cannon on a patch of green, a pyramid stack of tarred cannon-balls near the base of the pole where the Lone Star flag waved desultorily in the hot breeze, a rock-lined path. *Right fancy*, Taggart thought.

'You won't get much out of those prisoners,' he opined, lighting a smoke. 'They're too scared of Escalante.'

Buck Kirby packed his pipe to his liking, scratched a vesta along the wall and puffed until he had it drawing well. 'They're all Mexes. We'll get something.'

'Escalante's men don't talk, Buck. They know if they do they're as good as dead. Even jail won't save them. No witnesses, no charges can stick. It's how he's survived for so long. That and graft.'

Kirby frowned, rubbed the carved cherrywood bowl down the side of his nose, greasing it with the skin's natural oils. 'We don't need much. If we can get enough to have a judge sign a warrant, I'll be happy to take it from there. If I have one warrant, I can have it scaled up with a little more . . . er . . . evidence.' He paused and looked carefully at Taggart. 'You remember how it works?'

'Seen it work with others, way back, but Escalante's more powerful these days. He can call in the best legal advice in the country — hell, in the whole blamed world! He can afford it. Look how he thumbed his nose at *El Presidente* in Mexico City. He's still free — every assassin they've sent has gone home in a box or disappeared off the face of the earth. Don Diego'll be a mighty hard nut to crack, Buck. And he sure won't be happy at losing his load of guns — for the second time.'

'What he likes and don't like don't concern me.' Kirby shifted his big body in the chair; that wound in his 'back' was actually a little lower down — and almighty uncomfortable. But he wasn't about to admit he had been shot in the butt by some *peon*. 'I been told to say *gracias* for helpin' us out — and see if you care to stay on.'

Taggart paused with his cigarette half-way to his mouth. 'Join the Rangers permanently again?' He shook his head. 'Thanks, but no thanks, Buck.'

'You could come in as a sergeant. Wouldn't take long for someone with your experience to climb up from there.' It seemed to be hurting the Ranger to say this.

'Buck, I have a ranch to run. It's doing pretty good and Jimmy Morse is a mighty fine *segundo a mano*. I like ranch work and I have to keep money coming in regularly to pay for Rachel's care in that Denver school. I have a lot of expenses just keeping the spread operating.'

Kirby seemed mildly surprised. 'You gone through that reward money already?'

'I'm rich enough on the books, but ready cash is in short supply. Money's all tied up in the ranch. And a sergeant's pay in the Texas Rangers won't bring in enough ready cash. You know that, Buck.'

Kirby shook his head. 'Hell, we was sure you'd stay on.' He didn't seem unhappy that Taggart didn't want to stay in the Rangers. In fact, he was more than a little relieved.

'You put too much faith in that saying: *Once a Ranger, always a Ranger*, Buck.'

'Well, Captain Eadie wants to see you and thank you. Happen to know there's a kinda dinner arranged too.' Under his breath he muttered, just loud enough for Taggart to hear: '*Man gets lucky and they make him a goddam hero!*'

Clint glanced hard at him but he had more on his mind than Kirby's petty jealousy. 'Why the hell you let that happen, Buck? You know I don't care for those things. Hell, I'm getting outta here.'

'Sit down, you blamed fool. You know what Doc said about your leg. You can't ride within a week in case you bust that big artery. Hell, you were plannin' on bein' away on the original deal for a couple of weeks. Take the time anyway. You said Morse is a good man. Shoot the breeze with some of the old hands, fellers you used to serve with — '

'If you think they'll change my mind

for me about re-upping, you're wasting their time and yours.'

Kirby shrugged, spreading his hand. 'Eadie won't let you go without some sort of official 'thank you'.'

'We'll see.' It wasn't that Taggart was faltering in his resolve; it was that damn thigh wound that bothered him. It was *almighty* sore.

And, deep down, he was afraid he might do too much and cause the artery to burst and drain the lifeblood from him. He would rather have a formal dinner than *that*.

He had faced bullets, bayonets and cannon-balls with the Texas Brigade in the last year of the War. Afterwards, he had fought forest fires, floods, stampedes, Indians and rustlers — and he had been scared on many occasions. Wisely so, according to some veterans: a little, controlled fear was preferable to no fear at all. A man totally without fear was a dangerous man, usually ended up getting a lot of good men killed along with himself.

But this was different: he could kill himself just by trying to do too much too soon — cause his own death within seconds and there would be nothing anyone could do to prevent it. He had never faced such a problem before. He wanted to get back to the ranch, too, but . . . Maybe he should rest up a spell before travelling. But first he'd have to get this damn official dinner out of the way; he hated being the centre of attention.

He didn't know it then but that little quirk would decide whether he lived or died.

★   ★   ★

'This gringo *excremento* cannot be allowed to live!' screamed Don Diego Escalante, his whole body quivering, eyes rolling in their sockets. A small fist, flashing with gold and jewelled rings, thudded on to the edge of his heavy desk He raked those dark, hate-burning eyes, flat and cruel as a snake's, around the three men standing before him, heads bowed and silent. 'I want this gringo dead! Do — you — hear — me? He must die!'

He paused, thin chest heaving beneath his brocaded vest and silk shirt. There was a trace of spittle at the corner of his slit of a mouth. He seemed to be trying to find enough breath to continue berating the man who had killed his only son. He set his gaze on the tall Mexican who, wounded, had brought him the devastating news from the river crossing.

'Dolfo, I trusted you to protect Franco with your life!'

'I did, Don Diego,' the tall Mexican said huskily, his voice trembling slightly. 'I took this wound protecting him. But it was *caos* — *desordenarto*! You have never seen anything like it! I try to keep an eye on Franco but there are men riding here, running there, shooting, jumping or falling from their horses. The river was a mass of churned water and blood, bullets were flying . . . '

He let the words drift off as he watched the Don's long, narrow face slowly harden. 'You *tried* to keep an eye on my son, you say?'

Dolfo nodded vigorously. '*Sí*, Don Diego. I did my best, I assure you. I swear on the grave of my mother I — '

'Which eye?' Escalante asked softly.

Dolo stiffened. '*Perdon*, Don Diego? I do not understand.'

'A simple question, Dolfo. Which eye did you try to keep on Franco to see no harm came to him? You don't know? You are not sure . . . ? Well, I think it was — yes, the left one. It looks like a lazy eye and it did not do its work properly.' He flicked his gaze to the two Americans standing just behind Dolfo, the Wetherby brothers. 'Take him away and have Emilio remove that left eye.'

Dolfo jumped, started to yell protest. 'No, Don Diego! No! — I beg you . . . '

Milt and Mel Wetherby closed in fast, iron fingers gouging into Dolfo's arms as he tried to break away. He struggled and bucked and kicked, even tried to bite Mel on the wrist. Mel looked at his brother and nodded. Milt drew his six-gun and slammed the butt against Dolfo's bent head. The man's full weight sagged between them and they held him like a sack of laundry.

'See to it,' Escalante snapped. 'Then find this gringo assassin and . . . bring me his head!'

★   ★   ★

Buck Kirby got it wrong: the 'official' dinner was far from being that at all. It consisted of only half a dozen Ranger officers, Captain Eadie himself, and, of course, the guest of honour, Clinton Taggart.

'Relax, Clint,' Eadie said, pouring fine brandy into a glass in front of the uncomfortable-looking Taggart. 'Buck made it known to me that you would not — er — appreciate a formal event. I confess I'd forgotten your dislike for attention when you served in our ranks. My apologies. So I've compromised.'

He swept an arm around the long table where other men were sitting, glasses already charged. 'Your fellow Rangers from your time with us — all risen from troopers to their present status. You could've been one of them, but you chose otherwise — as was your right.' He grinned suddenly. 'Actually, it was Ranger regulations rather than your 'right' that forced you to quit, wasn't it? But that's as maybe. Now, gentlemen, let us drink to Honorary Ranger Clint Taggart. May he be on call whenever we need him!'

Taggart was embarrassed as they toasted him, Kirby hiding a scowl behind his tilted glass. 'Commander, I did nothing more than lead Buck's men to the part I figured the gun-runners would use as a crossing and, after that — well, it came down to a shoot-out and every man who was there deserves to be honoured, the dead as well as the living.'

There was a moment's silence, then Captain Lewis Carmody, who had trained with Taggart, stood up, glass raised. 'I agree with Clint, sir. Would you gennlemen be upstanding and drink to those who fought so well? I give you the toast: To the fallen, as well as the living!'

The men drank solemnly and then Eadie decided to do away with any remnants of formality remaining.

'Gents, food will be served in a few minutes. Let's put it out of the way quickly and then we can get down to a real celebration of a well-won victory, something the Rangers've needed for a long time — and a reunion among old friends.'

That was all it needed. Collars were unbuttoned, belts loosened, jackets removed and the anecdotes began to fly around the table, becoming more and more outlandish as the night progressed. Taggart had only a blurred memory of being helped back to bed in the Laredo barracks, emphasizing in slurred tones, that it was only his wound in his thigh making it so hard for him to walk straight.

'Sure thing, Clint,' said one of the burly Rangers holding his arm and winking at his companion on Taggart's other arm. 'Nasty wound, all right.'

'The — nastiest,' agreed Taggart, and come morning the only thing about himself he would have described as being 'nastier' than his thigh wound, was his throbbing head.

Hand shaking as he sipped a steadying drink, he glared at Kirby who seemed none the worse for the night's carousing. How could the man not be hung-over, damnit!

'I hate your guts, Kirby. I'm gonna leave word with my cowhands that you are to be shot on sight if ever you approach my ranch again.'

Buck Kirby grinned, feeling superior with his ability to absorb so much booze without a trace of hangover: *something* he was better at than that damn Taggart. 'You're outta practice, is all. But you've a whole week yet before Doc'll let you leave. We'll soon have you broke in again like in the old days.'

'You can go to hell. Never did like you, even as a sergeant.'

Kirby grinned wider. 'You've no idea how badly I regretted you weren't still in my troop when I made captain, Clint.'

Taggart looked across his raised, now-empty glass, smiled wryly. 'Guess I was a bit of a hell-raiser at that.'

'Till you met Lorene; she sure tamed you down.' Kirby realized he had hit a sore spot when he saw the way Taggart's face changed. *That* wouldn't help the man's hangover. 'Aw, hell, Clint. Didn't mean to stir things up . . . ' He didn't sound all that contrite, but he did mean the apology.

Taggart dragged down a deep breath and nodded, holding up a hand. 'It's OK. I can talk about her a lot more . . . calmly since I got that cougar. Guess focusing on that cat was my way of fighting the world for taking her away from me. I'll never forget her, Buck, never. But I can think about her now without that . . . withering feeling turning me inside out at just the mention of her name. Yep, she tamed me down. After she was killed, for a while there I didn't care what happened to me, then Red Wing jarred me back to reality by making me realize that Rachel needed me more than ever.'

'Guess we should never have asked you to lead us down into Mexico. It could've turned out mighty different. I'll see it don't happen again.'

Taggart spoke slowly, gaze steady. 'I figured I owed the Rangers something, Buck. Quitting like I did when I was offered that reward.'

'Hell, most men would've done the same. It was a hell of a lot of money.'

'Yeah, I guess. But I reckon I've squared things now and from here on in, I'm riding mighty easy. Rachel has to grow up without a mother, but she won't have to grow up without a father if I can help it.'

# 6

## Who is he?

Mel and Mitch Wetherby paused in the brush and timber just before the cleared run-up to the hacienda walls. They were both big men, wide-shouldered, features similar, though Mitch's battered face was the tougher. There was barely two years between them: Mel, thirty-one, Mitch thirty-three. They had grown up together, closer than most brothers, almost like twins at times, seeming to know just what the other was thinking.

Now Mel felt in his vest pocket and pulled out a battered quarter, the coin briefly flashing in the fading sunlight. He flipped it into the air, caught it on the back of his left hand, slapping his right hand over it swiftly.

'Heads or tails?'

Mitch paused, pursed his lips. 'Tails,' he hazarded, and swore when his brother uncovered the coin and George Washington's head stared up at him. He cursed as Mel laughed, putting the coin back in his pocket.

'You lose. You get the privilege of tellin' that crazy Spaniard that we cain't find out who the Ranger was that killed Franco. Who ain't any loss, you ask me. He was as loco as his Old Man.'

'Oh, howdy, Don Diego,' said Mitch looking past Mel's shoulder. 'Din' see you there at first . . .'

Mel almost tumbled from the saddle, he whirled so fast, face going grey. Then Mitch's harsh laughter rasped at his ears when he realized he had been had and his curse was both imaginative and blistering. He dropped a hand to his six-gun. 'By Godfrey, one of these days, Mitch! — One — of — these — days!'

Mitch yawned elaborately, patting a gnarled hand across his open mouth. 'Well, let's get it done.'

They rode on to the ground that was

kept cleared for fifty feet out from the hacienda walls, waved to the armed guard on top of the gated archway.

Minutes later they were ushered into Don Diego's office where the man sat like a small, vicious spider, hunched over some papers, lifting only his snake-eyes as the men entered.

They removed their hats, and Mitch ran a hand back through his lank, pale hair, pursing his lips and moistening them before giving the bad news.

'A whole damn week, Don Diego,' Mitch added after he had finished speaking and the Spaniard had said nothing, nor had he changed his expression, either in his eyes or on his long face. 'We looked everywhere, spent a small fortune buyin' drinks for off-duty Rangers . . . ' He paused hopefully, but Escalante made no mention of reimbursement. 'No one seems to know just who it was shot young Franco.'

'Someone did,' Don Diego hissed, sitting back in his chair now, making these big, tough *americanos* kind of queasy; this Spaniard could scare a rogue grizzly into throwing up. 'And I want to know who it was! I will learn this — and I will learn it soon or there will be others who will lose more than an eye!'

Mel cleared his throat, figuring he had better add his two-cents' worth. 'We figured that seein' as the Rangers won that fight at the river, that they'd have a kinda celebration, mebbe hand out a medal or two . . . '

Escalante looked surprised, and then even mildly pleased at Mel's words. 'That was very good thinking, *amigo*. It brought no useful information?'

Mel shook his head, growing more confident now at the Spaniard's milder tone and looks. 'No. Nothin' at all. No medals, no big booze-up. Just a small reunion was the closest it come to anythin'.'

Escalante's eyes narrowed and he leaned forward slowly. 'A reunion?'

'Yeah. Some ex-Ranger visitin' the

97

station got together with fellers he used to ride with. Wasn't much, accordin' to the feller I was drinkin' with. Just half a dozen and Eadie . . . '

'Commander Eadie?' Escalante was alert now, tense, his long-fingered hands clutching his chair's arms. 'He was there?'

'So this feller said, but it was just an excuse for a few drinks, you know? We gringos do that kinda thing.'

The Spaniard shook his head slowly. 'No! I do not *know*! And neither do you, my friend! If this 'visitor' was important enough for the Ranger commander to drink and carouse with, I wish to know who he is!'

Mel and Mitch both knew what was coming then and braced themselves as the Spaniard asked quietly, 'You, of course, learned this man's name? Where he was from? Why he chose to visit the Laredo Ranger station at just this time . . . ?'

The Wetherbys shuffled their feet, murmuring.

'What? I did not hear you — Mel . . . ?'

Mel cleared his throat. 'Well, no, Don Diego, we didn't bother askin' who it was. I mean, it was just some retired old coot gettin' a few free drinks in the sutler's with some of his old pards — '

'Oh? You know enough to say he was 'old'?'

Mel looked appealingly at his brother and Mitch squared his shoulders.

'No, I guess we don't *know*, like, I mean, we can't swear that he was an old retired Ranger, but — well, it stands to reason, Don Diego.'

'It stands to nothing!' roared the Spaniard, on his feet now, slapping a hand flat on his desk top, scattering papers, his eyes burning. 'It stands to your incompetence! You come here before me and say you have 'done your utmost' to carry out the task I gave you, and it turns out you have done absolutely *nothing*!'

'Aw, well, you can't really say that, Don — ' began Mel, trying to sound reasonable. But he flinched when Escalante shouted,

'*Silencio*! You are fools! Like all gringos! I should have your tongues torn out by their roots!'

That was too much for the brothers; with one thought and one slick movement they whipped up their pistols. Don Diego reared back in shock as the hammers cocked.

'Now, *señor*, we know you are a mean-assed cocksparrer, and you can do what you like with your greasers, but you are talkin' here to a couple of genuine sons of Texas, and you start talkin' about rippin' out eyes or tongues to us — well, you gonna die, feller. Right now, if you try it on!'

Mitch was looking as mean as he ever had and Mel looked mighty dangerous, too, ready to shoot. Sweat running down his face, Don Diego dropped back into his chair, waved a hand. He drew a silk kerchief from his sleeve and dabbed at his damp face, shocked into temporary silence. Then:

'My apologies, *amigos*. You must understand, Franco was my only son, and to a Spaniard an only son is the most important thing in the world. He is the one who will inherit the family, the one to guide them, protect them in the future, bring them honour, put to good use the efforts of the father . . . An *hidalgo* like myself is devastated if he loses that child.' He even essayed a slight, cold smile. 'I am beside myself with grief. I am hard, even cruel, because the world has treated me cruelly! But — yes, you are right. I should not threaten you with punishments I would mete out to my *peons*. You are gringos and your ways are not my ways . . . But I must have vengeance! I must learn the identity of my son's murderer!'

He stood again, looking somehow smaller than before. He wiped his mouth with the silk kerchief. 'Gentlemen, who is he? Who is this man who has killed Franco? I charge you to bring me this information. And this time you shall have the added incentive of reward. Shall we say, a thousand *pesos*, in gold . . . Each?'

Mel and Mitch Wetherby exchanged glances, and at the exact same moment they smiled and holstered their six-guns.

'You got yourself a deal, Don Diego,' they said in unison.

They left minutes later and Don Diego sat hunched in his chair, glaring; he would not forget that small humiliation! He would devise a more . . . fitting 'reward' than *pesos* for these *gringos* who dared hold their guns on him.

He heard the door in the other wall open and turned towards it. A young woman in riding-clothes, carrying a plaited quirt and a pair of small leather gloves came in smiling. She was long-legged, and pinch-waisted, her embroidered silk blouse tucked tightly into a wide, embossed leather belt, showing her mature breasts straining at the cloth.

Her face was oval, longish like her

father's, but where his mouth was pinched and slashed, her lips were full and ripe, her nose petite, dark eyes flashing, her head surmounted by raven hair that reflected stars of light from the windows. He stood and, smiling, the movement of taut muscles softening his stern face only a little, held out his arms. She came into them and, slightly taller than he, bent to plant a kiss on his cheek.

'Ah, Consuela, you grow more like your mother every day! She was the beauty of Mexico City society before we had to . . . leave, but I think perhaps you are even more beautiful.'

She laughed, tightened her arms briefly then stepped back. 'That is a fine welcome for any woman from her father!' She sobered and lightly slapped her quirt into the gloves she carried in her other hand, dark eyes sliding to the main door. 'I saw the Wetherbys leaving . . . '

The query was in her voice and he shook his head slightly, sober again, sitting down. 'Nothing! The fools have learned nothing. I think now, though, they have a lead that may produce the information I require, but — '

'*I* will find him! I will find this *cabrón* who murdered my Franco!'

His jaw sagged at her use of the epithet and his face darkened. 'Consuela! You will not speak this way! I will not have you using . . . '

She waved his words aside and he was so surprised at the gesture that he stopped speaking.

'I loved Franco! In many ways he was foolish, but he tried hard, *very hard*, Papa, to live up to the standard you wished for him!' Her eyes became wary for a moment, but she made a visible effort and kept on. 'Perhaps a standard too high for him to attain — but he was afraid of you, afraid to fail! He — might still be alive today if you hadn't — '

She reeled as his hand slapped her brutally across the face. Tears sprang to her eyes and she stood there, quivering now, even cringing a little, her own fear evident. But then she shook herself, tossed her head.

'I should not have said that, Papa. I apologize. You will forgive me? Please, Papa?'

He made the effort, forced himself to calmness and embraced her, stroking her hair. 'Of course, *chiquita*. I, too, am sorry, but you must never — never say such a thing again.'

'I — I am so upset about Franco . . .' She sobbed and he tightened his grip, gave her his silk kerchief, sat her down in a chair.

'I know, *querida*, I know. I do not have a lot of faith in the Wetherbys, but I do believe that this time they may have success. Some success, anyway.'

Sniffling, she dabbed at her eyes, glanced up. 'If they do not, Papa, will you — will you allow me to look for this murderer? I would be so proud to do something to help avenge Franco.'

He regarded her soberly and her moist eyes did not waver. He knew she had fire and commitment — and courage, a lot of courage. She could ride well, shoot well, had been trained since she was a little girl to protect herself — and she had that fire of the *conquistadores* in her blood, that resolve. He realized he was now searching for the things in her that he would have wanted to find in Franco — and why not? She was his hope now, for the family honour, the family's future.

Under his guidance, perhaps, she would meet his requirements.

'*Sí*,' he said quietly. 'You will have your chance, Consuela. I have already ordered that this murderer's head be brought to me but — '

'No, Papa!' she interrupted, hands tugging at his sleeve. 'No. He does not deserve to die quickly and cleanly! Let us prolong his life a little — a lot! And make it as painful and as miserable as we can devise.'

Slowly, Don Diego Escalante smiled. 'I was wrong, *chiquita*. You do not grow more like your mother each day. You grow more like me!'

She stared at him for a long moment, then smiled dazzlingly, coming forward to grasp both his hands in hers, dropping the gloves to do so. She squeezed with her fingers tightly.

Her bosom was heaving as she dragged down deep breaths of emotion.

'Papa — Papa! I am honoured that you compliment me so! And I swear to you on the Holy Mother that I will find Franco's killer and I will make him suffer the tortures of the damned, writhing, slobbering for mercy, before he is finally allowed to die! This I swear!'

She clutched her heart and he tried to keep the surprise from his face.

*Dios mio*! She even frightened him with her intensity.

# 7

## The Hunted!

'His name's Taggart, Clint Taggart. He has a ranch north of San Antonio, somewhere near the Edwards plateau.'

Mitch Wetherby looked at his younger brother, then turned his attention back to the sowbelly and blackened beans he was cooking into a revolting mess in a skillet thick with burned-on grease from many previous meals.

'How much did it cost to find that out?'

Mel hitched his hip on to a rock and began to build a cigarette. 'Well — best part of a five-spot.'

'Hell almighty! What'd you do? Buy the whole damn bar whiskey and beer chasers?'

'No, you don't savvy how it was, Mitch.' Mel fired up his cigarette, exhaled a plume of tobacco smoke to join the clouds rising from the skillet. 'You're burnin' the grub. Yeah, well there were two off-duty Rangers in the bar and I had to go easy, you know, what with them dodgers on us. They're old and we look different without our beards but — anyway, I bought beers all round, then when they started to relax, steered the talk around to the reunion. Neither were at it, bein' new. 'Joined after that Taggart'd left,' one said and I cocked an ear. 'Taggart?' I asked him — '

'C'mon! C'mon! Judas, you take all damn night to tell a story!'

'All right! They talked about the reunion, jealous as all hell that it was a private party. I had to buy whiskeys and more beer, and keep buyin' 'em! But finally got it out of 'em. This Taggart was the guest of honour.'

'You're sure?'

'Damn right. He's got a knife-wound in the thigh an' all.'

Mitch snapped his head up and

whistled softly. 'Well, that kinda clinches it, all right. Diego's men said the kid managed to stab the feller in the leg just before he was shot. Where is Taggart now?'

Mel's face fell. 'We've missed him. He pulled outta Laredo yest'day or the day before. They couldn't agree on when. Seems he was hired as a guide, but used to be a Ranger.'

Mitch swore. 'Now he's headin' back home?' he asked as he scraped out the burnt mess on to two scratched tin platters. At Mel's 'Guess so', he said, 'Then we pull out come daylight. He'll likely follow the railroad camps on that new line they're buildin', skirt Choke Canyon reserve, and pick up the San Antone trail from there. Might even cross the reserve. Save himself some miles.'

'And keep him a long way ahead of us!'

Mitch, forking some charred grub into his mouth and trying not to grimace at the taste, snapped: 'So? We don't pick up our *pesos* from Diego if we don't kill this Taggart.'

'He won't be no pushover if he was once a Ranger.' Mel poked around at the food on his plate, losing the appetite he'd had when he first rode in and smelled the savoury bacon. 'You think Diego meant it when he said 'bring me his head'? Judas, I ain't never cut anyone's head off. Dunno as I'd want to.'

'Me neither,' Mitch admitted. 'No, we shoot him and lug his body back to the hacienda. Let Escalante or one of his greasers do what they want with him.'

Mel seemed relieved. 'Yeah! Good idea. You know, Mitch, I don't mind cookin'. I'll take on that chore from here on in, if you like.'

'You sayin' I don't cook good?' Mitch bristled.

Mel straightened from scraping the mess off his plate behind a bush. 'No. I'm sayin' that what you served up to me ain't even attractin' that starvin' coyote watchin' us from near that greasewood.'

'You lookin' for a whippin'?' Mitch half-rose, still chewing, challenging, and Mel held up a hand quickly.

'Not me. What I'm lookin' for is a cup of java, unless you burned the water when you made it.'

Mitch blinked, then suddenly grinned. 'You smart-mouth little sonuver! Just as well I'm in a good mood or I'd kick your butt till your nose bleeds.'

Mitch Wetherby always felt good when a killing was in the offing. It was the kind of chore he liked.

★　★　★

The Ranger sawbones in Laredo had given Taggart the OK to ride, adding the proviso, 'Just don't push it too hard, Clint. Take as many breaks as you can; travel short distances, rest up. Try not to do too many miles in the one day.'

Taggart said he would watch it and he intended to. The leg was healing well but it still felt kind of stiff and was sore. The medic had told him he could expect this soreness for at least another week; it would gradually diminish during that time.

Commander Eadie shook his hand and told him he might call him into service again if the occasion arose.

Taggart shook his head. 'I felt I owed the Rangers this one, Commander. I'm a rancher now. Full stop.'

'Aw, Clint, you don't mean that. You got Ranger blood in your veins, you'll have it the rest of your life. You'll be glad of the offer to work with us, take my word.'

Taggart didn't feel like arguing so he just smiled, adjusted his hat and walked out into the yard where his sorrel and packhorse waited. Buck Kirby came out of the shade of the *galeria*. He was glad to see the rancher was leaving and would dearly have liked to know what had been said between him and Eadie just now, but he nodded curtly and thrust out his right hand; they had breathed a lot of gunsmoke together. 'Ride well, Clint. We be seeing you again?'

'Not unless you come up to the ranch or pass through the cattle yards at San Antone.'

Kirby felt relieved and widened his grin. 'Commander didn't try to have you stay on, then?'

'He tried.'

The grin tightened some. 'And you refused?'

Taggart knew Kirby was probing and merely shrugged, stepped up into the saddle and settled on the sorrel with a grunt of pain. He rubbed his left thigh.

'Still actin'-up?'

'Doc says to take it easy and I aim to. *Adios*, Buck.'

'Not *hasta la vista?*'

Taggart grinned and shook his head. 'Relax, Buck. I won't be giving you any competition. I ain't reupping.'

Kirby reached up, grinning a mite sheepishly. 'Ah, I know. Just me. Always been edgy about such things. But the

Rangers owe you one now, Clint. Don't forget that.'

Taggart turned and led his packhorse out of the Laredo station. 'Think I'll just try and stay outta trouble.'

'Hey! That's the kinda advice we Rangers give civilians!'

Taggart laughed. 'Oh, yeah! Think I remember . . . '

Now it was two days since he'd ridden out and his leg was giving him trouble. Nothing to lay him up or make him think about abandoning his journey, but he couldn't get it comfortable, either riding or at night in his bedroll. Doc had told him to keep a light bandage over the wound and to beware of any show of blood. So far there was no bleeding or pus and he began to relax, decided it was the muscle healing more slowly than he had expected. As long as the wound stayed free of infection, he could put up with the endless ache in his thigh muscle.

But it gave him a limp and he wasn't happy about that. He needed to be able to move fast and smoothly working his ranch, and any wilderness trail was dangerous and might call for a fast run for cover.

He saw the smoke from one of the railroad camps just this side of sundown and decided to make for it, spend the night there. The workmen usually welcomed a stranger for his company and fresh news and conversation. And he felt like a little company himself.

He was right: they were glad to see him. The cook supplied him with a massive supper and the men broke out some firewater they had concocted and made in a still put together from railroad copper pipe. It was potent and Clint said so, but held out his tin cup for another belt. The men cheered.

'You must be a genu-ine son of the Lone Star to back up for seconds of this mankiller!' the foreman said, a tough ranny with an Irish accent. He squinted at Taggart and asked, 'Your name wouldn't be . . . Taggart?'

The cup lowered and Taggart's face

was wary as he nodded slowly. 'Clint Taggart.'

The railroad men were suddenly silent, exchanging glances Clint couldn't read.

The foreman swigged some firewater. 'Had a couple hardcases stop by right after noon — bought some of this rotgut and kinda casual-like, asked if we'd seen a big feller with a limp goin' by the name of Taggart.'

Clint waited and the foreman heaved a sigh. 'Likely nothin' wrong, but — we — none of us — liked the look of 'em. Buzz there, said he thought they were a couple outlaws he'd seen a dodger on once.'

'Was a deputy sheriff for a spell in Witchita Falls,' Buzz explained. 'Been thinkin' on it, and I reckon they was named Wetherby, brothers. Wanted for murder, as I recall. Train hold-ups mainly, but anythin' to turn a fast buck.'

All eyes were on him now and Taggart spoke slowly. 'I was a Ranger once. Think I recollect the Wetherbys.

Never met 'em, though the name rings a bell.'

'We-ell. Don't want to get you all edgy,' the foreman said, 'but the boss come up from the big camp south of here where the main supply dump is, and he mentioned them two stoppin' by and askin' about you there, too. Day or so back.'

'I didn't stop at the big camp, rode wide, and made the river crossing on the horse-ferry, saved some riding.' He unconsciously tapped his game leg. 'Which way'd the Wetherbys go?'

'Right up the track, so I guess they're goin' on to Camp Eleven. We can let you have some grub so you won't need to stop at Eleven, can give it a wide berth.'

'Thanks, friend, but I have enough supplies to get me where I'm going. Obliged for your warning.'

'You pullin' out now?'

'Reckon I'll get me a good night's sleep, leave before sun-up, so don't worry you hear someone moving around that early.'

'Hell, Cooky'll be lightin' his fire. You speak to him nice, he might even find you a cup of coffee for the trail.'

But Taggart slipped away from camp in the dark, about an hour before sun-up, forgoing coffee, his rifle across his thighs, making sure it didn't rest on his wound.

He had no idea why the Wetherbys might be after him, but he recalled that old dodger he'd seen when he was riding with the Rangers. They were killers, hired out for dirty dollars, had a bad reputation, but he hadn't heard of them in years.

In the distance, he could see the gleam of the newly laid rail track, drifted his gaze around until he saw steady smoke lifting in the distance. He figured this would be Camp Eleven; it held no attraction for him. He was a long way from it here, now turned towards the line of low hills with their sparse cover of brush and timber. As a Ranger he had camped in there at an

Indian well that not many whites knew about.

He had been riding for three hours now and his leg was throbbing, so he figured to locate that old well and rest up some. Just to be on the safe side, he wouldn't light a fire, although he craved hot coffee.

Still, as he recalled, the well-water was sweet and cold. It would see him through and he could top up the canteen there, save another stop to the north.

It took a half-hour to locate the well again after all this time, but he found it, sat his sorrel amongst the thickest stand of timber and watched for a spell. Birds came down and chattered and fluttered and drank and splashed at the edges of the water. A bobcat slunk in, wire-taut edgy like all wild things exposing themselves, and drank quickly, yellow eyes roving restlessly, then streaked back into the rocks.

It seemed safe enough: birds and animals wouldn't go in and play and drink if they figured man was around someplace close.

So he rode the sorrel out slowly, rifle ready, turned loose the packhorse to go drink and crop some grass, then slid out of the saddle.

The jar of landing rammed up his leg and brought a grimace of pain, but it was only momentary. He took his saddle canteen, uncorked it and sank it below the surface of the dark, tea-coloured water. It tasted of vegetation but was sweet and cold as he remembered. Taggart sat on a rock, rifle beside him, canteen between his feet, and twisted up a cigarette.

Then a rifle crashed and the canteen leapt wildly, water spraying all over his lower legs as the bullet tore through the metal beneath the cloth covering.

Taggart rolled to the right, scooping up the rifle before the second shot thundered — the bullet coming in from the other side this time, sending his hat spinning. He landed heavily and scrabbled awkwardly behind the rock.

His leg was stiff and didn't want to move without causing him pain, but he dragged it out of the line of fire and huddled close to the rock, rifle hammer spur under his thumb. Two guns: it had to be the Wetherbys, playing for keeps.

'The only way to play, I guess,' he murmured as he glimpsed a flash of sunlight off blued metal, angled to his right. He could pin-point the place where the rifleman was almost exactly by that single flash. To reach the gun barrel, the sunlight had to slant in past a crooked tree-trunk and he could see the small pile of rocks almost hidden behind some brush. *Number one located* . . .

As he started to look for the second man a rifle fired again and a bullet whanged off his shelter. He ducked but looked through a gap between two of the rocks, saw the shroud of powder-smoke rising from the explosion.

And number two was right underneath it.

Both killers now located, he swung

his own rifle up, butt firm to shoulder, settling his right cheek to the stock — just as the man over there under the gunsmoke lifted slightly for his next shot. Taggart fired a fraction of a second before the killer and he saw the rock dust spurt, a rifle barrel cant wildly against the sky as the man either fell back or was driven back by the bullet. Number one rifle sent two bullets whining off his shelter, making him duck, rock chips flying.

He dropped down between the rocks as number one fired a third shot, still aiming at the higher position. Clint Taggart beaded him swiftly, the old Ranger discipline locking in so that even with speed, he still squeezed the trigger, didn't jerk and thereby throw his aim.

His aim was good and a man yelled, reared up, exposing his head, shoulders and chest. Taggart's Winchester kicked against him and the man over there spun as though he had been roped and yanked off his feet. He tumbled over the rock, slid down out of sight.

A large smear of blood glistened on the sandstone.

'Mitch!!' yelled Mel from his cover. 'Goddamnit, answer me Mitch!'

There was no reply. Mel cursed aloud and, careless of his own safety, exposed himself and emptied his magazine at Taggart's shelter. Clint ducked and had to stay ducked as the bullets raked and spattered and ricocheted, showering him with rockdust and leaves shaken from the shading branch above.

He rolled out from behind the rock, landed on his belly, worked trigger and lever, got off four fast shots. He saw all four hit the rocks. He dropped the now empty rifle and twisted on to his left side so he could get at his Colt holstered on his right hip.

He rolled on to his wounded thigh and the pain was like a fist taking him on the side of the jaw, rocking his whole body. The world disappeared behind a bright curtain of flaring yellow light and he fumbled the six-gun. Operating by pure instinct, he caught the heavy Colt and got off two shots, holding the trigger depressed, thumbing the hammer each time.

He fell forward then and lay there, unable to move for the paralysing pain riding completely up his left side.

Through the roaring in his head he heard the drumroll of galloping hoofs and a voice drifting in across the shuddering waters of the well.

'Mebbe not this time, Ranger! But I'll be back for you, you murderin' son of a bitch!'

Using his elbows and knees, Taggart dragged himself in behind the rock again. He thumbed home two shells to replace those he had fired, closed the cylinder, looked around warily. He could still hear the retreating horse — but was there a man on its back? Or had the horse been frightened into running, riderless, driven out by Mel Wetherby, so as to give Taggart a false sense of security?

After a while, he eased up and was able to climb atop the rock. He could see a little way out on to the flats. There was dust drifting up from the chaparral — then he saw the horse. *And its rider!* Making for the cover of the hills.

So that left the man he had shot off to his right.

He took his time approaching, limping in an awkward crouch, coming in from behind. Mitch Wetherby was down and there was a lot of blood as he lay slumped against a boulder, head at a crooked, awkward angle. His blood-smeared hands were empty, palms up, in the dust. The rifle, with a splintered fore-end, and the six-gun lay well out of reach.

Taggart took time to fully load his rifle, watching Mitch from cover all the while, but the man barely moved, his ragged, harsh breathing like wood being sawed. Rifle cocked, Clint limped in, stood looking down at the dying man, Winchester covering him.

'Don't recall your face, Wetherby.

Must've had a beard on the dodger when I saw it.'

Mitch's drooping eyes fluttered half open. The blood-flecked lips moved several times before any sound came.

'Mel . . . ? My — brother . . . ?'

'Run off — left you.'

Mitch almost smiled. 'Knew I was — done.'

'Why the hell you after me?'

Mitch just stared for a long time and Taggart repeated the question twice. Eventually Wetherby's eyes opened fully and he said,

'You are — one unlucky — sonuver-bitch! You killed — Diego's only — son . . . ' This time his upper body shook with laughter but it lasted only a few seconds. Then a gout of blood spewed from his mouth and Taggart stepped back hurriedly as the man slipped over on to his side and died.

So that was it. Diego Escalante was after him.

And the man had enough money to hire a whole damn army if need be to make sure he avenged the death of his son.

Well, if Eadie was right about him having Ranger blood, the odds were about right — if you believed that old adage: *One riot, one Ranger.*

# 8

## Sniping

Mel Wetherby waited in a small cutting he knew, sure that Clint Taggart would appear, taking this short cut to bypass the Choke Canyon reserve.

He waited in vain.

He cursed loud and long, laid his rifle aside and changed the crude dressing on the wound in his chest. Well, not actually *in* his chest: the bullet had passed between his upper body and arm on the right-hand side. There was a lot of blood and not inconsiderable pain but he had just about managed to stop it bleeding now. He emptied the remains of his flour sack, shook it until most of the dust had gone, then tore it into strips and used this to bind a fresh pad over the gouge.

It hurt, but it wasn't serious, he knew

that. What was serious was Mitch's death. He felt that a part of himself had died back there in the ambush they had so carefully rigged once they realized they were ahead of Taggart. They hadn't allowed for his leg wound slowing him down but when they had, leaving railroad Camp Eleven, they figured it was all to the good: they could set up an ambush ahead now.

Huh! It had been the worst thing they could have done, the way it turned out. That damn Ranger, ex-Ranger, whatever the hell he was, was just too damn good for the Wetherby boys.

'Never even got to bury Mitch proper,' he complained aloud, realizing by this time that Taggart must be riding through Choke Canyon, and not skirting it.

Well, it wouldn't save the son of a bitch! Mel wasn't worried about Escalante or his cut-throats or anyone else now. *This was personal*! Between him and Taggart.

If he could nail the bastard before he

reached his spread, he would gladly lug the body back to the greaser — maybe even cut Taggart's head off, and hand it to Diego on a plate and demand his 1,000 *pesos* in gold. More he thought about it, the more he liked the idea of making a profit. Mitch would approve.

'Don't waste your time and energy, boy,' Mitch would say. 'You aim to kill Taggart anyways, so do it, collect the bounty and live it up.'

Yeah, that was the thing to do. He could buy Mitch a real good headstone. He stopped dead in his thoughts. Damn! That was the one thing he couldn't do! Mitch likely wouldn't even have a grave, thanks to Clint Taggart. He would have been left to feed the coyotes.

The surge of hatred and impatience to get started on his vengeance actually made him feel faint.

'By hell, Taggart, you dunno what sufferin's waiting for you!'

*  *  *

Red Wing had kinfolk in the Choke Canyon reserve. It wasn't really an Indian reservation: there was the lake which in future years would become a reservoir, feeding many small towns along the unpredictable Nueces River. But in this year, when Taggart rode through, there were only surveyors and an Indian encampment around the lake.

Taggart found Red Wing's cousins and nephews and nieces and rested up for two days, leaving just after mid-morning on the third day. The oldest squaw, a medicine woman, had massaged his thigh with some reeking salve she had made from rendered-down deer and groundhog grease mixed with herbs and ground burn-bark, topped off with dried snake-liver.

He turned his head away each time she used it but those knowing, knobbly fingers found the knotted tendons and muscles, eased them apart slowly. White-ash powder and arnica were rubbed into the extensive bruising that still showed and after the two days of intensive treatment he was surprised to find that he could walk now with barely a sign of a limp. There was just the sensation of pressure on the inside of the thigh, mainly when he was riding, but this was nothing compared to what it had been.

The squaw insisted he take some of the salve with him and he accepted it reluctantly, well-wrapped in deer-hide and the intestines of a wild pig. He left some money and rifle cartridges with the Indians and emerged to the north of the large lake. In another two or three days he would be home.

* * *

He reached the L Slash C on the third day, around noon, and Jimmy Morse came hurrying out of the barn, hands and forearms black with grease from working on the front hubs of the buckboard.

'Welcome back, boss. I guess you

ain't so pleased to be here that you'd want to shake hands right now . . . ?'

'Think you've growed smarter while I been away, Jimmy, observing a thing as subtle as that.' Taggart swung down easily from the saddle but there was just a slight stiffening and a momentary pause as his left leg touched the ground. The smile disappeared off Morse's face.

'You been hit.'

'Almost healed now.'

'My God! Where'd you sleep recent? In a bear's den with him lyin' dead alongside?' Jimmy wrinkled his nose and Clint grinned. 'Man, that is one real gen-u-ine *stink*!'

'Real Kiowa perfume.' Clint waved the ball-like package of salve and Morse stepped back another pace. 'Guaranteed to work.'

'That pong'd wake a dead man! You ain't gonna eat at the same supper-table as the rest of us, are you?'

Another cowhand came up, calling 'howdy' to Clint. He unsaddled the sorrel and then started on the pack-horse, while Taggart and Morse walked back to the barn. Clint hung the salve ball from a wire and hooked it on a high nail but the foul odour still drifted down. Morse cleaned off the grease with kerosene and then scrubbed hard with lye soap, asking questions all the time.

Taggart gave him a very condensed version of things and Morse looked concerned when he had finished.

'I've known of Escalante. Worked on the Rio freight boats for one season and the skipper made a little extra *dinero* by carrying some contraband for that Mex. Guns and somethin' else, never did find out what, but I know for a fact one time it was a man, someone on the run. Escalante is a real mean one. Glad you're finished with him.'

'Not quite. Seems I killed his only son during the fracas at the river.'

Morse snapped his head up, mouthed an oath. 'Hell almighty, Clint! That ain't a good thing! Those fanatical old

Spaniards live, eat and breathe nothin' but family! He'll send someone after you for sure.'

'Already has,' Clint said and told him about the Wetherbys.

Morse looked out towards the distant hills and swept his gaze right around. 'I've heard of Mitch and Mel Wetherby, too. You're in more trouble than Custer, Clint, except you won't see yours comin'. And you'll never know when.'

'Point is I *know*, Jimmy. I can prepare for it.'

'You bring the men in on this, Clint. You'll need 'em and they'll stand by you to the last man.'

Taggart wasn't sure about this; it was his problem and he didn't want to involve any more of his cowhands than he had to. But common sense won in the end and he agreed that it would be stupid not to advise the crew.

'How about the Rangers?' Morse asked. 'You was workin' for them when you got into this bind.'

'They're stretched to the limit as it is, Jimmy. Oh, they'd do something if I asked, but they don't have enough men to handle their own problems. I'll handle this all right.'

Morse put his hand on Taggart's arm. 'Don't underestimate Escalante, Clint. He invented meanness. He's the orneriest son of a bitch I've ever heard about.'

'You known me all these years and haven't noticed my streak of meanness, Jimmy? Hell, man, it's a mile wide when I want to call on it.'

Morse was not amused. His face and voice remained serious. 'Don't joke, Clint! Please, *amigo*. You think you've seen hard times before, but they're nothin' compared to what this snake can pull — an' that's gospel.'

Taggart frowned, disturbed, yet touched by Morse's concern. He nodded soberly.

'I'll take care, Jimmy. You have my word.'

Jimmy Morse nodded but he didn't seem any happier.

Buster Harris was the first.

He was the L Slash C wrangler and was working in Morning Canyon, bringing in the ranch horses that had been allowed to roam the range for exercise and to have a change of feed.

The horses knew him and the hardy little paint he rode and most were co-operative, but there was always the teaser, the comedian, who had to go through his little act. He would come with the other small bunch, answering Buster's whistles and shouted commands, and then, when about to enter the big canyon on the home range, would suddenly break away, neighing and bowing its head, mane blowing. Challenging Buster to come chase him and bring him back.

Harris was doing this, good-naturedly, for he had a genuine love of horses, and although he cussed and swore there was no real heat in his words.

This time it was the strawberry roan:

it hadn't acted up for some time so he was caught more or less by surprise. The roan led him down the slope and along a wild animal trail no wider than a chair seat. Buster had to fight his paint as it struggled to keep a fast pace along such a narrow strip and while he was hauling rein on the approach to an elbow bend the bullet hit him and lifted him out of the saddle.

He was still in mid air when he heard the rifle's report, but it didn't do him any good. The lead had taken him high, between the shoulders, and even as he fell to the brush-covered ground he was starting to lose consciousness. The paint slid off the trail, panicked some, whirled away down slope through the clawing brush.

Buster hit hard and, only semi-conscious, reached instinctively for his six-gun. It was a ponderous, groping move, evident to any watcher that Buster was past being any kind of danger.

It didn't stop Mel Wetherby from

putting two more bullets into him, knocking him flat, the Colt half-drawn.

The echoes cracked and died away and after a while Mel rode down on his trail-stained claybank, rifle butt on his thigh, hand on the action. He didn't know Buster Harris: had just been watching him for the past day or so, figured where he would be working his horses and had lain in wait. Now he dismounted and went through the wrangler's pockets, taking a few coins, a good Buck folding knife and a neatly folded blue silk kerchief with the initials 'A.H.' hand-embroidered on it. They stood for Angus Harris and had been lovingly sewn by Buster's elder sister who lived in Salt Lake City.

It appealed to Mel Wetherby and he unfolded it, shook it out and made it into a neckerchief, which just fit his thick neck. The paint came scrambling up from the slope now and without hesitation Mel shot it through the head. He took ammunition and what he could use from the saddle-bags, then removed Harris's spurs and put them on, tossing away his own bent and rusted ones.

Humming to himself he walked along the trail, saw that it led across a gully and into a canyon where the other horses were gathering around a rock pool of permanent water.

He mounted again, tested the wind, smiled when he found it was blowing in the direction he wanted, then dropped several burning matches into the brush as he made his way back along the narrow wild-animal trail. The fire might not trap all the horses but some would die.

And that was fine by him.

One way and another, Clint Taggart was going to lose a lot more stock before Mel put a killing shot into him and took him back to Don Diego.

★　★　★

'It was cold-blooded murder, Clint. Buster was shot in the back and then the killer gave him a couple more in the chest to make sure.'

Taggart's face was grim as he listened to Jimmy Morse's pronouncement. He turned to where a couple of sober cowboys stood by their mounts. 'Wrap Buster in his blanket and tie him on to one of those broncs.' As the men obeyed, he turned to a third man who came struggling up the trail, blackened with soot, coughing. 'How bad, Muddy?'

'Counted four dead, Clint. Five others burned too bad to save.'

Taggart nodded. 'I heard your shots. The rest?'

'Seem to've made it out that zigzag cuttin' at the rear of the big canyon. One down there with a busted leg and he was trampled some. I'd say he fell and near-blocked the cuttin' but the others were so scared by then they just stomped all over him to get by.'

'Christ! Whoever did this is a heartless damn son of a bitch!' gritted Morse, scratching his head. 'Can't abide any slaughter like this.' He moved his eyes to Taggart's hard face. 'Reckon it's that Wetherby brother?'

'Be a good bet. Dunno much about him, but as I recall the Wetherbys were wanted for murder and ranch-burning. Be his style.'

'Never left no tracks worth the name, Clint,' Muddy Waters allowed. 'He was smart enough to drop his matches behind him so when the brush burned it wiped out his tracks.'

The rancher was standing with hands on his hips, looking around at the mountains, slightly hazy still from the canyon fire. 'He's up there somewhere. Likely got the glasses on us right now, watching our reaction.'

'You see the sun flash from his lenses, let me know!' Morse said, levering a shell into the rifle he held, jaw jutting.

Taggart drew his six-gun and fired four spaced shots into the air, startling his men. Standing in a cleared area, on a slab of sandstone, he turned slowly, holding up the smoking Colt, touching it, then touching his own chest, finally

143

stabbing a pointing finger up the slopes — telling Mel Wetherby he was coming after him.

There was no reaction that anyone could see. Taggart reloaded the six-gun as Jimmy Morse asked, 'Reckon he saw?'

'Yeah. He's watching. He saw all right.'

'You going after him now?'

'No. He'll be long gone and well hidden before I get up there. He wants to hit us again — and again and again — before he decides to square off. I killed Mitch and he wants to get his own back and make sure I know it's him before he comes in for the kill.'

'Well, hell, we don't have to take that! We got a big enough crew to scour these hills till a gnat's fleas can't hide from us.'

'I reckon he won't stand still while we search, Jimmy. And if we leave the ranch empty . . . '

Morse frowned, nodding jerkily. 'Yeah! Wasn't thinkin', Clint. But,

Judas! You're lettin' him dictate the terms!'

'No choice right now, Jimmy. Everyone's gonna have to keep their eyes open, post a guard while doing their chores. Won't be a lot of fun, but I'll figure something meantime.'

And Jimmy Morse knew what that would be: Taggart would go after that killer, wouldn't endanger the lives of any of his men. He'd work out what Wetherby was doing, where he showed or left sign, figure a pattern — then he would go in there after him.

Alone.

# 9

## Closing in

Morg Callow was the next to be shot from ambush.

A young, hard-working cowboy, Taggart gave him the responsibility of bringing in the small herd of 'specials' they had stashed earlier on the prime grass of a high-walled gulch — it was too small to be called a 'canyon', although the local name for it was Antelope Canyon. Long ago a few of the small agile Texas antelope had made this their home but both red man and white had soon decimated the population.

Taggart's best beef cattle were here, fattening, undisturbed, with plenty of succulent grass and sweet water. These were the beeves he hoped would bring the big money that would subsidize a lower price level on the rest of the herd. Some were good enough for seed-stock. All told there were about twenty, and a man as good in the saddle as Morg Callow would have no trouble driving them down to home pastures. The sale would bring Clint some much needed cash.

But Mel Wetherby was a man with an eye for good beef stock, gained from years of rustling; also, he and Mitch had grown up on a west Texas ranch and had been worked like slaves by their father. He followed Callow when he left the ranch alone, followed him right into the canyon and recognized the plump beeves for what they were.

He let Callow bunch them together and then shot the man out of the saddle from a rock ledge. The shot crashed and echoed around the high walls and set the cattle to snorting and bellowing, starting to jump around edgily. Mel grinned and stood, watching, and was about to loose off a few more shots to start the herd moving when Morg, hit bad but not aiming to die just yet, dragged his pistol free of leather and got off a couple of shots of his own.

It took Mel by surprise — he figured he had nailed Morg dead centre — and he spun as rock dust spurted beside his head, ducked and dropped to one knee. He lurched as Morg's second bullet clipped his left ear and blood ran warm and thick down his neck. The rifle jumped to his shoulder and he quickly triggered three more shots. Two hit home, driving Morg down for keeps, the third ricocheted and found a home in the side of one of the lead cattle. It bellowed and rammed into the one next to it. They were already mighty nervy now with all the gunfire, and in seconds there was a concerted bawling, a clashing of horns and the unmistakable snorting thunder of a stampede in the making.

Holding his new blue neckerchief over his bleeding ear, Mel Wetherby grinned tightly as he watched the beeves jostle and trample each other trying to squeeze through the narrow neck of the gulch. One went down and didn't get up as its companions surged over it. The bellowing was magnified and pitiful.

Mel left the dying animal in its agony and clambered back off the ledge, dropped down a steep slope and leapt into his saddle. He cut through brush, the horse protesting to no avail, blood dripping from the spurs by the time they had burst out behind the running cattle.

Mel had moved around this area mighty carefully and thoroughly the last few days and he knew there was a small bog in a patch of marshland in a tight bend of the river.

Just big enough for this herd to flounder in.

He rode in close, kicking the leaders the way he wanted them to go; he figured there had been enough gunfire and maybe it had already been heard by other cowboys working the ranges. He wanted these beeves stuck in the mud and dying before any of Taggart's hands appeared.

They might not have heard the gunfire, this being in a lonely part of the ranges, but he didn't want to take that chance.

★  ★  ★

The gunfire from Antelope Canyon had been heard all right, by Taggart and Jimmy Morse, who had been riding a couple of ranges away, checking out the pastures. Some they would leave ungrazed so that they were rested, giving the grass a chance to rejuvenate for next season. The other pastures would be used for grazing this season's cattle; it would be their turn to rest next year.

The rattle of gunshots was unmistakable, flat and distant. The men were in different areas but knew where the gunfire had come from. Jimmy Morse swung his mount, headed out to find Taggart who was visiting the tranquil glade where Lorene's grave was, the cougar's hide still draped over a low branch of the tree that shaded her last resting place. There was a simple headstone that he had laboriously carved with her name. He cleaned this down so that moss growth would be delayed, and removed the few weeds, using his canteen to water some of the wild flowers with which he had edged the grave. He sat a spell, smoked a cigarette, and in his mind, spoke with Lorene, telling her of recent occurrences. Some might think him foolish, he knew, but it comforted him and he always felt better for having 'talked' with Lorene.

He knew that the urge to visit here would fade with time but, until it did, he was happy in the short periods he was able to spend here.

That was when he heard the first rifle shot, the slapping echoes disrupting his thoughts. He stood quickly, head cocked, listening. There came another couple of *cracks*! and he could distinguish them as being from a pistol. The rifle fired a short volley and he started for his horse.

'Have to go, Lorene!' he threw over his shoulder and for the first time he raced his mount out of the glade. Until then, it had been a place of peace and he had always dismounted and led the horse in quietly.

But something told him this was urgent.

Jimmy Morse was coming up the trail to meet him. 'You hear that? Antelope Canyon, I reckon.'

Taggart nodded and weaved past the foreman who was already turning his own mount to follow.

Now they were coming down into the hollow between the ranges and they could see the passage made by the stampeding herd.

'Judas! The swamp!' Jimmy yelled but Taggart was already cutting through the brush and up and over a hogback.

They were too late.

The beeves had been rammed full tilt

into the marsh, and were already up to their bellies, some managing to withdraw a leg only to sink down again, trapping all four legs. The men had their ropes out and whipping through the air in no time. The horses balked at the edge as soon as they felt the soft, muddy soil giving way under their weight.

'Get your loop over this critter!' Taggart yelled and Morse hurriedly wound in, tossed his loop again. It landed over the horns of the animal Taggart had already roped. They turned their trained mounts, rumps to the bog now, spurred away. The massive, well-fed weight of the steer pulled the horses' hindlegs down, an angry whickering bursting from their straining lungs.

Taggart swung out of the saddle as the rope looped securely around the horn, and flung his weight on the taut strands, muddy water being pressed from the woven grass fibres by the strain. Jimmy Morse did the same and with both men and horses pulling, they broke the suction and the bellowing beast floundered and skidded to the edge. It fought to get to its feet and Taggart had to dodge the raking horns as he freed the rope loops.

Immediately they lassoed another and fought and strained and heaved and brought this one skidding over the surface on its side. Panting, muscles aching, Taggart's thigh starting to throb and protest at the violence of the chore, they staggered, covered in mud, more spraying on to them as they coiled their ropes and picked their next target.

Then three cowboys came racing in, skidding their mounts. Taking in the scene at once they unshipped their lariats and joined Taggart and Morse in rescuing as many of the cattle as possible . . .

In all they saved seven; thirteen died, more than half the specials. Jimmy Morse shook his head dolefully, but Taggart said nothing: there was no need for words. Clint's hand trembled a little as he wiped mud from his fingers and managed to twist up a cigarette, looking at the carcasses lying in the mud, some with just legs sticking up in the air, or long horns pointing skyward, clogged nostrils showing.

The trio of cowboys had heard the shooting and had come arunning. Now Clint sent a man up to find out what had happened to Morg Callow in Antelope Canyon; deep down he already knew what the ranch hand would find.

The returning cowboy's face confirmed his worse fears. 'Morg's hoss had been horned, so I had to leave the body there for now, boss. Covered him with a blanket and some brush. Three bullets in him, like Buster.'

'Has to be Wetherby, Clint,' opined Morse.

'I should've gone after him right away,' Taggart said to no one in particular and only half-aloud. 'I was too damn eager to start getting the herd ready for the railhead. Too damn confident that I could figure his plan and beat him!'

Taggart had seen Tate McLaine, the sheriff, after Buster's death, had told him the story, and that he wanted to take care of it himself.

Tate was a middle-aged man who had been badly wounded a few years previously, while tackling a gang of bank-robbers on his own. The town, in appreciation, had kept him on as full-time lawman, even though he was really past being able to administer and enforce the laws of the land. But he had a good deputy, Woody Turner, who did most of the work. Tate was an old friend of Taggart's, knew of his past Ranger work, but was still reluctant to allow him to handle the situation.

'Woody'll look into it when he gets back,' the sheriff had told him. 'He's down sortin' out some trouble between the railroad gangers and the Chinee labourers. When he gets back I'll send him out to your place. I appreciate your Ranger background and such, Clint, but we gotta do this by the book.'

Taggart understood. Tate couldn't get around much on his crutches so the next best thing was to administer the law to the letter, ensure it was carried out so folk could see he was no one to mess with, crutches or no. Then no one could say he wasn't doing his job. And he would be able to keep his job, which paid a whole lot better than the pension he should have been on after sustaining his injuries.

So far Woody hadn't appeared and they heard that there had been a riot with some Chinese being killed and strung up by their pigtails. All of which kept Woody Turner mighty busy — and away from his home county.

'I can't wait for Woody any longer,' Taggart told the group out by the swamp and the dead steers. 'I'm going after Wetherby to put him in the ground.'

'Tate won't like it,' warned Morse.

'Hell, he can't do it. Woody's still away. It's gotta be done and I'm the next best thing.'

He winked slightly and Morse shook his head uncertainly. 'Tate can be mighty cantankerous these days, Clint. Even on pay-days, you never know whether he's gonna shake your hand and tell you to go sleep it off or throw you in the hoosegow and fine you a week's pay for gettin' drunk.'

'Yeah, he done that to me,' grumbled Leech, one of the cowboys.

Surprisingly, Morse snapped, 'How'd you like to go from bein' a respected town-tamer and champeen square-dancer to hobblin' about on crutches? Judas, it'd turn a saint ornery!'

The cowboy looked surprised and shrugged. 'Well, he still done it,' he said, sullen now.

Morse wasn't paying attention. By now he was watching Taggart. 'You better take a few men with you.'

'We're short-handed as it is, thanks to Mel Wetherby. You keep the hands working, Jimmy. I'm going back to the ranch and get cleaned up. Then I'll hit the trail.' Clint turned to a tow-headed cowpoke who went by the name of Snow. 'You were an army scout once, you told me, Snow.'

'S'right, boss. 'A' Comp'ny, Eighth Cavalry, under Cap'n Prescott Early.' The man was still mighty proud to have served under the popular and highly decorated Captain Early.

'While I'm getting my gear back at the ranch, scout around and find me all the tracks you can. I want to know where Wetherby was headed. His campsite would be fine.'

'Sure, boss. How about I meet you up on Broomtail Butte yonder an' I can give you all the details?'

Taggart nodded and Morse tried all the way back to the ranch to talk him into taking at least two or three men with him.

'I've lost enough men because of Mel Wetherby, Jimmy. He wants me, so I'll go in alone. If he gets me, he'll leave. If I get him — problem's over and done.'

'You're a tough man, Clint. Just hope

you're tough enough.'

'Only one way to find out.'

★　★　★

There was a tall man with a black leather patch covering his left eye waiting when Taggart and Morse rode into the ranch yard. He stood and stepped forward out of the shade of the porch roof and they saw he was Mexican.

'Expectin' someone from *mañana* land?' Morse asked warily.

Taggart shook his head, watching the man watching him. The Mexican lifted a hand briefly.

'*Hola, señores* — You are *Señor* Taggart?'

The man was looking directly at Clint and Clint got the notion that he knew damn well who he was talking to: he hadn't even glanced at Morse.

Taggart walked his weary mount closer and Morse dismounted by the corrals. Keeping his horse between him

160

and the Mexican, Jimmy loosened his six-gun in its holster. Taggart folded his hands on his saddle horn, taking in the tall, lithe Mexican and the single big gun worn on his left hip, high and with butt foremost. *Cross-draw man*.

'I'm Taggart, mister. Who're you?'

The man smiled; he had a face that would appeal to women, the eye-patch lending him a rake-hell look. 'My friends call me 'Dolfo'.' The smile widened. 'It is not seemly to say what my enemies call me.'

'Well, guess a man has to have his enemies as well as his friends. What can I do for you, Dolfo?'

The Mexican grew sober and he leaned his forearms on the porch rail. 'I come on behalf of . . . another.'

Taggart had already felt a tingling in his whole body at sight of the man: the old in-built warning system stirring his defences to readiness. 'Who?' the rancher asked bluntly.

Dolfo tugged at his left ear-lobe. 'My employer. He lives some distance to the south and he extends an invitation to you to visit his *rancho*.'

'I got no time for socializing, mister. This is a working ranch and the season is moving right along. I suggest you do the same.'

Dolfo smiled again, spread his hands. 'I will do as you ask, *señor*, but the invitation is still open. It comes from my *jefe*, Don Diego Escalante.'

Taggart felt the electric shock through his guts but he had suspected it somehow, in the back of his mind. He shook his head.

'I got no business with your boss. Can't think of any he'd have with me.'

'Ah, but he has, *señor*. There have been certain . . . happenings along the border that have affected Don Diego's business and family interests. He has heard that you were involved in these . . . incidents.'

Taggart said nothing, waited the man out. Dolfo's confident smile tightened a little. 'At the river crossing at a place not generally known but used by Don

Diego's men at certain times. Some call the place De Carreteras.'

'I've heard it called Diablo de Carreteras — the Devil's Crossroads.'

Dolfo's smile disappeared altogether and his single visible eye slitted. 'So, you know what I am talking about! You were there!'

'I've been there.'

'You were there! When the Rangers struck!'

'I was once a Ranger.'

Dolfo almost laughed, cut it short. 'You are what you gringos call 'stonewalling', eh? A name somehow complimentary to one of your generals, I think . . . And you are very good at it, my friend, but, as in all good poker-games, I have cards that will trump your ace. Is that how it is said?'

'Near enough. Come on, Dolfo. Spit it out. What's Escalante want with me?'

The Mexican nodded slowly, the single eye regarding Taggart almost with a touch of respect. 'They said you are tough, unafraid. But, if you will take my advice, *amigo*, be afraid! A touch of fear is often good for a man.'

Suddenly Dolfo stiffened as Taggart's right hand lifted, holding his cocked six-gun, the barrel unwavering on the Mexican's chest. 'You talk a lot and say nothing, Dolfo. Time to answer my question: what does Escalante want with me?'

Dolfo was mighty leery now, held out one hand, half-lifted towards his head. 'Easy, *señor*, easy! Don Diego wants to kill you, for murdering his son, Franco.'

Taggart frowned. 'I already know that. The Wetherbys have been harassing me. Mel still is, but I shot Mitch a while back.'

'*Dios*! I did not know that.' The Mexican pursed his lips. 'You are more dangerous than we knew! But Don Diego grows impatient.'

'Did Escalante think I'd ride back with you to his hacienda knowing he wants me dead?'

Dolfo's face grew cunning. '*Sí, señor*, he expect that.'

'He must take me for a damn fool.'

'Ah, no, Taggart, no! He does not do that. He knows you will come, because he knows you will want to see your daughter. Rachel, I think, is her name? She is a guest of Don Diego at this very moment.'

# 10

## Bloody Trail

They were far into the hills now, Taggart riding a little ahead of Dolfo. The Mexican sat easily in the saddle, his big, heavy gun in its holster but his eyes alert.

Taggart had his guns, too, his Colt on the cartridge-belt around his waist, his Winchester in the saddle scabbard.

Only thing was, neither gun was loaded.

After Dolfo had delivered his shattering remark about young Rachel, Taggart was frozen in both body and thought.

*Rachel — kidnapped! By that devil Escalante . . . ?*

His mind could not grasp such a situation, coming out of the blue as it did. His cocked six-gun sagged to the side unnoticed, and Jimmy Morse, watching from the corrals, stepped quickly around his mount, his own pistol in hand now, hurrying towards Taggart.

Dolfo saw him and, outwardly calm, held up a hand.

'Do not be foolish, señor! If anything happens to me, you will never see the child alive again. This I promise you.'

Morse hesitated, stepped up beside Taggart and looked at his grey, drained face. 'You say, Clint.'

The ramrod's voice seemed to break the spell and Clint's frown deepened as he flicked his gaze to Morse, then back to the relaxed Mexican who was lighting a cigarillo.

'Leather the gun, Jimmy. There's some talking to do here.'

Morse obeyed and the Mexican shook out the match, flicked it into the yard. 'No, Taggart, we have said all we need to. You will accompany me back to Don Diego's hacienda and there you will see your little girl. I must make certain . . . checks along the way, you understand. If I don't . . . ' He paused, shrugged his wide shoulders. 'Then there will be no need for you to continue, because . . . Ah, but you are a man of the world. You know how these things work.'

Smoothly he drew his gun, a big, heavy Le Mat, a French revolver with an upper and lower barrel. It had been converted from percussion to centre-fire and was a cumbersome but deadly weapon; it held ten shots: nine .41-calibre bullets and the smooth-bore under-barrel fired a .66- calibre shot-shell. The gun had a kick like a Missouri mule with colic. Taggart found himself looking at the selector on top of the backstrap; it was set to the left, meaning Dolfo could fire the shot barrel if he squeezed the double-action trigger. It was as deadly as a sawn-off shotgun at this range. He stiffened when Dolfo jerked the barrel.

'Very carefully, señor, you will shuck the bullets from your Colt, then empty the rifle's magazine. You, too, Señor

Morse. Please! I am not so patient by now and if I kill you right here, Taggart, it may displease Don Diego a little, but as long as I take him your head I think he will forgive me.'

He was in control and knew it: so did the gringos.

They both obeyed. Then Taggart said, 'How do I know you have Rachel? You got something of hers to prove it?'

Dolfo laughed briefly. 'No! I have nothing to prove the truth of what I say. Just take my word for it, Taggart: your little girl will die if you do not co-operate. Can you risk that? If you doubt me because I cannot produce some proof, and I cannot . . . ' He gave that expressive Mexican shrug again, 'then you will certainly lose your only child.'

'Jesus, Clint!' breathed Morse. 'This — this is a real lousy deal!'

Taggart's eyes were as deadly as the black maw of a cocked pistol when he told the Mexican, 'You don't give me much choice, so I'll ride with you,

Dolfo. But you may not make it all the way. Think of that.'

Dolfo no longer looked amused. 'You fool! You kill me and your child is dead!'

'See,' Taggart continued, 'I'm wondering just how much Don Diego would care if you were to be killed. I mean, you let his only son get shot at the river. He can't think all that much of you.'

'Take it easy, Clint!' hissed Morse. 'He's loco! He'll shoot you here and now!'

'No, Dolfo doesn't really want to do that. Well mebbe he does *want* to, but I don't think he'd like to have to tell Don Diego he killed me when Escalante must be really looking forward to getting his hands on me himself.'

'God almighty, you take some chances!' Morse said.

But Dolfo looked bleak and murderous. 'You will come with me, Taggart! You have no choice.'

*And wasn't that the truth! Unpalatable though it was.*

Clint turned to the worried Morse. 'He's right, Jimmy I have to go. You carry on with getting the herd together. Listen, I heard that that horse-breaker, Buck Kirby, is back in Laredo. He's damn good. Send him a wire, tell him we need his talents. See if he can help us out.'

Morse caught on quickly enough, nodded jerkily. 'Yeah, well, if Buck's pockets are empty I guess he'll be lookin' for work — '

'Offer him top money. We have to get that herd on the trail.'

'Enough!' Dolfo snapped suddenly. 'It is time to go.'

★   ★   ★

Now Taggart and the Mexican were riding through the hills and the rancher was looking out for Snow, who ought to be waiting at Broomtail Butte by this time. The riders would look normal enough; even if Snow didn't recognize the Mexican, the fact that Taggart was leading the way and carrying his weapons would put his mind at ease.

Taggart was even a little afraid that if, for some reason, Snow was suspicious, he might pick off Dolfo from his ledge, and then it would mean the end for Rachel when the Mexican did not make his expected check-ins along the way.

'How did Escalante know about Rachel?' Taggart asked, not turning his head, but knowing his words would carry easily to the tall Mexican.

'Don Diego knows many things, señor. He reaches into many places; his gold buys him anything he wants. If the gold does not work, then he has a reputation, that will almost certainly bring co-operation.'

'If he harms Rachel . . . '

Dolfo laughed briefly. 'What could you do?'

The words were enough to silence Taggart; it was a question he was unable to answer.

Yet . . .

But he was working on it.

Then Snow, mounted on his big dappled white horse, waved from the ridge. Dolfo asked quietly, 'Who is the man with the white hair?'

'Cowhand. Name of Snow. He was looking for tracks left by Mel Wetherby.'

'Tell him to go about his ranch work.'

'He's . . . ' Taggart was going to argue but decided it would be safer if Snow did not come any closer. He called, 'It's OK, Snow — This man with me knows Mel and his hangouts. He's taking me to one right now.'

Snow, obviously mystified, didn't answer right away. 'You want me to ride along, boss?'

'No. You go back and see Jimmy Morse. He'll find a chore or two for you.'

Snow was close enough now for them to read the puzzlement on his long, horse-like face. His gaze was on Dolfo who smiled and nodded in friendly manner.

'*Hola, amigo* . . . Mr Taggart say you are one fine tracker, eh? But I know where this Mel is and — '

'Then why the hell you takin' the boss in the wrong direction?' Snow's query was tight and very suspicious. 'I found tracks leadin' the other way.' His hand drifted towards his gun-butt.

'No, Snow, don't . . . ' called Taggart but his words were drowned in the thunder of the Le Mat's shot barrel and the spray of lead pellets shattered Snow's chest, flung him awkwardly and violently from the saddle.

Taggart spun his mount, rammed it into the Mexican's horse, leaving his saddle at the same time, hurtling at Dolfo. The Mexican was taken by surprise and lifted his smoking pistol, triggering. But he had not moved the selector across to the cartridge barrel and nothing happened.

Taggart's head drove up under his chin and together they sailed through the air and landed heavily on the edge of the narrow trail. The loose-packed earth gave way and they went over, sliding and rolling down the slope, tearing at each other, striking wildly. The Mexican was strong and clubbed at Taggart's head with the heavy pistol. He missed, but the cylinder of the Le Mat clipped Taggart's shoulder and he felt the numbness clear down to his wrist. He pronged his fingers and stabbed at Dolfo's face, only then remembering the leather patch. One finger found the edge of Dolfo's only eye and he jerked back wildly. The other finger tore the leather patch free, revealing the raw, puckered flesh of the empty socket. The Mexican growled and butted Taggart in the face. His nose creaked and blood flooded over his mouth and chin. He jerked his head aside as the big gun swung at him again, passing through his thick mat of brown hair, scraping his scalp. It burned and stung and he hooked an elbow under the Mexican's jaw. The head snapped back and the gun fired: Dolfo had pushed the selector lever across. It urged Taggart to fight harder, faster, more violently. He got a knee into the man's belly as they skidded and half-rolled on to a flat area.

Dolfo kicked, catching the rancher on the hip, just above the thigh wound. It hurt and for a panicky moment, Clint thought the scar might break open and the lethal blood-flow would start. But he didn't dwell on it, wrapped an arm about Dolfo's leg and held tightly, threw himself backwards. Dolfo yelled as he was yanked violently forward and over Taggart's falling body. He crashed into some brush, the dry branches tearing at his face. This slowed him down, for he was a vain man, had taken a long time to adjust to the empty eye socket but decided the leather patch, worn in the correct manner only added to his attraction to certain types of women. But he did not want scars disfiguring him, too, and in a savage rage, he reared up, turning, kicking again. His boot caught the incoming Taggart on the side of the jaw.

The rancher dropped, fire and lights

bursting inside his head, pain wrenching through his neck and face. The world went out of focus and spun in blurs, and then the heavy gun's twin barrels slammed across his head and sudden night fell, without stars or light of any kind. Only exploding pain.

★　★　★

He lay there without moving, feeling his ravaged senses slowly returning. It took a lot of will power to remain entirely still, eyes closed, waiting for his hearing senses to give him some idea of what was happening around him. He heard a match scrape, smelled strong aromatic tobacco smoke: someone was lighting a cigarillo or cigar.

It came back to him then. Dolfo, the man with the leather eye-patch — and the ultimatum about Rachel.

The memories hit him so solidly that despite himself he snapped open his eyes — and saw the Mexican sitting on a round rock, staring directly at him.

'Ah, you join the land of the living again, *señor*. I was afraid I might've hit you too hard. This Le Mat — its weight can crack a man's skull like an overripe melon. I have seen this happen.'

He said the last with a tight grin. There were superficial scratches on his face but his patch was now covering his empty eye-socket again. 'You are lucky, I think.'

'Mebbe one of us is. Don't feel like it's me.'

Dolfo laughed. 'Ah, I like you, Taggart! They tell me you are tough man. I think it is true.'

Taggart sat up slowly, somewhat surprised to find that neither his hands nor his feet were bound; but his gun belt was gone. He looked up from examining his wrists and the Mexican shrugged, spread his hands.

'Is all right. You will not give me any more trouble.' He sobered, adding, 'My apologies for killing your *amigo*, the man with the white hair. He left me no choice.'

'You didn't give him a chance — not with that shot barrel.'

'He would've killed me, you know that. *I* was the one left with no choice.'

Taggart frowned: the Mexican sounded as if he really was contrite. But that was crazy . . .

'One thing — you sure got that damn cannon out faster than I would've figured.'

'Practice, *señor*, practice. I was Franco Escalante's personal body-guard. That is why Don Diego was so . . . displeased when I failed to protect Franco.' He touched his eye-patch automatically. 'Thanks to you!'

'I always heard he was a mean son of a bitch. Now you want to make it up to him, huh? You've got to deliver me to him so he can make me suffer plenty before he kills me, right? And you hope this'll get you back in his good books.'

Dolfo's dark eye narrowed. 'So, you realize this, eh? You are smart as well as tough.' He paused, took two long, thoughtful drags at his cigarillo, blew out the plumes of smoke at an angle without taking his gaze off Taggart.

'Perhaps — perhaps we can make a deal. You and me, Taggart . . . A deal to our mutual benefit?'

Taggart was very still now, stunned, but trying not to show it, though he thought he wasn't having too much success, for Dolfo smiled slowly, almost mockingly.

'That surprise you, eh? Well, allow me to explain and you can think about it.'

All Taggart could think about was Rachel; truth was, he didn't know what the hell to make of this one-eyed Mexican. The man said some crazy things, jumped around like a bee hunting nectar, but there was some kind of underlying . . . resentment? Anger? Hatred . . . ? None of those seemed too exaggerated. There was *something* sticking in his craw and despite his claimed loyalty to Don Diego Escalante, Taggart suspected it might not be quite as clear-cut as it seemed.

Now the Mex killer was offering to do a deal!

He had no idea what it could be but he was willing to listen — as long as it didn't further endanger Rachel.

'So. What do you figure could be to our 'mutual benefit', Dolfo?'

'Ah, you are sceptical. You are smart, but not smart enough to see what I could possibly suggest that would put us both on the same side.'

'You're right there, mister. Damned if I can. But you're going the long way round the mountain. Why don't you cut through the pass and get right to it?'

Dolfo seemed mildly puzzled but nodded. '*Sí*, I take a long time to get to the point, because I am still thinking about what I will say. This was not planned — but now that I have met you, I think I see a way for us both to get what we want.'

'All I want is for Rachel to be safe.'

'Of course. This is what I have in mind. First, I did not protect Franco as I should and he died. For this I am sorry. But for *this* . . . ' he touched the leather eye-patch, 'I am even sorrier!'

'I can savvy Don Diego not being happy with you for letting his son get killed.'

'Of course. That I understand also. But this thing he do to my eye, it is the kind of punishment he give to one of his *peons* who have displeased him! Me — Adolfo Ybarra de Santiago! I have hidalgo blood in my veins, too. Oh, not pure like Don Diego, but some. Four years I am Franco's protector. I save him from much trouble. To do this I kill people, women as well as men. Once I burn a town so he can escape with a whole skin. Sometimes I am wounded and once I nearly drown dragging him from a river where one of his wronged women had staked him out so he will die slowly . . . ' His face was changing now with the memories. Taggart sensed a rising self-pity in the man: he was truly hurt by Escalante's treatment of him. And it was slowly eating him away.

Now Dolfo mashed out the cigarillo

although it was smoked only half-way. His lone eye drilled into Taggart.

'I have been dealt with wrongfully, Taggart. I am a proud man and my pride has been badly damaged!' He touched the leather patch once more. 'I have much pain, many headaches, to remind me of my humiliation! I see in others' faces that there is no longer any respect . . . ' His nostrils, caked with flakes of dried blood from the fight, flared. 'And this I can not, will not, accept. I have been dishonoured and the matter must be put right.'

Taggart was growing edgy and impatient but tried to keep it from showing in his voice; this Mexican could jump one way or the other right now. He could lose his temper and shoot the rancher on the spot and to hell with the consequences if he thought Taggart wasn't taking all this as seriously as he wished. 'What did you have in mind, Dolfo?'

'Revenge! Of course, it must be revenge, bloody revenge! My honour could not be satisfied with anything less.'

'I see that, but what do you want to do?'

Dolfo thought about it a little more. 'Franco had a sister, Consuela, a haughty, fiery *señorita* of eighteen years, now her father's favourite. She has always been much loved, I suppose, but like all the old Castilianos his first thoughts and expressions of regard had to be for his son. Now Franco is dead, and I must tell you that Consuela loved him dearly. Naturally, she wishes to replace Franco in her father's affections, to have Don Diego's full favour.'

He paused and there was the beginning of a sly smile as he said quietly. 'So she make him an offer: he wants to kill you, to make you suffer a time of hell on earth, for shooting Franco. So she offers to help. She will go to the Denver school where your child is, pretend she is an aunt or cousin, and bring Rachel back to the hacienda. The child will, of course, be used to bring you to Don Diego.'

Taggart remained silent but his brain was seething.

Dolfo smiled when he read Taggart's face correctly. 'Naturally, you wish to kill her for bringing such danger to your child. So, we will ride in together to Don Diego. It will appear to be the best thing ever for that *cabrón*!'

'And . . . ?' Taggart's voice was barely audible.

'Well, he will be too elated to suspect anything and you will then do your part, Taggart. You will kill Don Diego.'

'Why don't you do it?'

'I will help if need be; certainly I will keep Consuela from interfering, but I think you are the only one who can kill Don Diego. Believe me, he knows me too well, reads my thoughts almost before I know what I myself am thinking! But his mind will be so consumed with his hatred for you that he will never consider that the guns you carry are actually loaded . . . ' He paused and gave that expressive shrug.

'And it wouldn't be good if they found your special calibre bullets in Don Diego's body, would it, Dolfo? They'd gut you like a catfish ready for the camp-fire.'

The Mexican's single eye glittered, his face tightening. 'Ah! We could make a fine team, you and me, Taggart!'

Clint ignored that. 'Suppose your plan works up to that point. What happens after I kill Escalante? There'll still be Consuela and any other guards he has in the room. Most important of all, as far as I'm concerned, there'll be Rachel, in the same room as flying bullets, and then we have to escape from the hacienda — The whole scheme needs more work — I won't try it the way it is: it's too dangerous.' And yet, it might be the only way he could save Rachel.

The Mexican's face was sallow and hard. With a vicious curl of his thin lips, he spat, 'Then prepare to watch your daughter die before your eyes, Taggart! That is what Don Diego proposes, anyway. And *then* prepare yourself for a death that will make the tortures of the Apache look like the games of children!' He drew in a hard breath, single eye glittering. 'Or, your other alternative: you can die right here.'

Taggart smiled, shaking his head. 'No, Dolfo, that's one thing I don't have to worry about. You need me. The plan needs refining and we have to do it together. But I'm in a position to make some demands. You see that?'

The tall Mexican was sullen and his lips pursed, jaw jutting as he glared at the rancher. He badly wanted to kill Taggart right then but he knew he couldn't do without him if his plan for revenge was to be successful. There was no other way.

And Taggart had not yet thought of the obvious: that the *only* way it would work so that Dolfo could save his own neck, was for him to kill Taggart immediately after the rancher had killed Don Diego.

*That* would make him a hero again,

restore his honour.

And, if Consuela should step into the way of a stray bullet — all would be well! *Blame it all on Taggart.*

Dolfo smiled suddenly. 'We will work together on this thing — to our mutual benefit.'

Taggart doubted that last part but he nodded slowly. Dolfo might see this as the only way he could take his revenge on Escalante, but Clint Taggart saw it as *his* only chance of escape — for himself and Rachel. It wouldn't be easy, but it was the only way he could see right now.

Then a third element abruptly entered the picture.

Mel Wetherby stepped out of the brush, his sawnoff shotgun covering both men as he ran his bleak gaze from one to the other.

'Well, gents, seems I arrived just in time. Figured it was that hand-cannon of yours I heard earlier, Dolfo. But you *hombres* . . . With a little thought on my part, you two can help me boost the bounty Don Diego's offerin' four or five times. All I gotta do is tell him what I just heard! Now, lift 'em high, boys, or I'll spatter you all over the mountain like that whitehead lyin' up on the ridge.'

# 11

## Silent Death

Now the odds were increasing — and Taggart didn't even have his gun.

He lifted his hands out slowly from his sides and, Mel, seeing he was unarmed, gave his attention to Dolfo.

He should have been watching the Mexican from the start. Too late he realized that, as Dolfo's hand streaked across to the bulbous butt of the big Le Mat. But, sitting as Dolfo was on the rock, even though he tried to stand quickly, the large gun was awkward to draw, the fat cylinder and heavy double barrels dragging on the crimped leather.

Wetherby was a fast thinker and whatever he had in mind must have included Dolfo staying alive, at least, for now. For instead of firing the scattergun he lunged for the Mexican, who stumbled when he tried to stand, the Le Mat's snagging pulling him off balance. The shotgun barrels swung at his head. He twisted away wildly, but they still struck his shoulder, numbing his right arm.

He staggered, abandoned his attempt at drawing his pistol, grabbed at the shotgun. He got a partial grip, yanked but pushed it to one side. One barrel fired and Taggart jumped back as buckshot ricocheted from saplings and rocks. On one knee, he watched as Mel Wetherby bared his teeth and hauled savagely on his shotgun. It came free of Dolfo's grip and Mel went down to his knees. The Mexican lashed out at his head with a boot, kicked the gun down the slope and slugged Wetherby where his neck joined his shoulder.

Mel was a long-time brawler, had been brawling all his life. The blow might have put down another man, but all he did was shake his head, eyes reddening with rage as he lunged up, grappled with Dolfo, trying to crush him with his thick, knotted arms. The Mexican had one arm free, stabbed at Wetherby's eyes with his thumb. They were teetering on the edge of the slope now, straining, intent on each other.

Clint Taggart ran forward, arms spread, caught both men around the neck and rammed a knee upwards. It caught Mel in the crotch and Clint hammered a blow into Dolfo's face, shoving hard all the time.

With a mingling of wild yells, both men went over the edge, struck the loose earth and rolled on down. Scrabbling and kicking and punching, they broke apart and Mel lunged for his shotgun that had landed only a couple of feet away.

On the edge above, Taggart spun and ran for his tethered horse. He slapped the reins free from under the ground-hitching rock and leapt into the saddle, spurs raking.

Crouching low over the arching neck, mane whipping across his eyes, Clint raced away from the bench. Someone was yelling. The shotgun thundered but he didn't hear the whistle of any shot. A six-gun hammered two fast shots, then came the deeper walloping sound of Dolfo's Le Mat.

Time to be a long, long way from here, he decided, jabbing with the spurs again, urging the sorrel on into heavier brush. Low branches slashed at him, tore his shirt. He just caught his hat in time, jammed it on tightly. The rifle-butt was under his left leg but its magazine was totally empty: Dolfo had seen to that, checked it personally.

He had nothing he could fight back with, so flight was the only option. Luckily he knew this country well. If he couldn't shake these two in an hour, he deserved to be an easy target for their bullets.

He was too confident. It seemed to him that Mel Wetherby, in his plan to harass the L Slash C, must have scouted this country very well indeed, made himself familiar with the range before starting his campaign of terror.

Every time Clint looked around, he could see a small dust spiral rising above the brush or timber. It was too large for one horse, about right for two. So he figured Mel and Dolfo had settled their differences for the moment and were putting a joint effort into tracking him down.

Now that he was alerted, he took more time in covering his trail. Once he took so long he heard Mel calling to Dolfo on a trail below the slope where he was erasing his tracks.

'If he keeps on this way, he'll end up in a ravine that's cut by a shallow stream. No easy way through but he'll likely ride up the stream to try to cover his tracks. If that jug-head of yours can make it, there's a way round the base of this butte an' with a little hard ridin' we can be waitin' when he comes out of the ravine . . . '

'My horse can easily stay with yours, señor!' Dolfo snapped back and Taggart heard Mel's harsh laugh before silence fell.

Obviously they didn't realize just how close they were to Taggart. But now he was alerted and his confidence had taken quite a beating. He knew where he had to go. Forget the ravine — Mel had outguessed him there, all right. He would ride straight up into the high country.

Where Red Wing's burial cave was, scoured by the winds that whistled through the crags.

And where he had left the flatbow and arrows beside the old Kiowa's corpse to accompany him into the spirit Land.

'Sorry, *compadre*. I still have use for that bow.'

★　★　★

'Goddamit! Where'd he go!'

Mel Wetherby asked it as a rhetorical question, looking about him as he sat his sweating mount on a narrow trail that swung across the steep face of the mountain. 'He's vanished like smoke in a rainstorm!'

'You guessed wrong, Mel, that is all,' Dolfo smirked.

Wetherby glared at the smug Mexican. 'You could do better, I s'pose?'

'Perhaps not, where tracking is concerned, but . . . maybe in another way. *Sí*.'

Mel frowned. 'Quit talkin' that damn greaser style, goin' round everythin' you say the long way! You got a notion that'll help, spit it out.'

Dolfo smiled maddeningly. 'Anger only confuses things *amigo*.'

'I ain't your damn *amigo*!' Mel raged. 'You got somethin' or you just talkin'?'

Dolfo narrowed his one eye at Wetherby's tone. 'I . . . have 'something'. I must make my check with certain people or Don Diego will assume I have failed and he will send men to find out what has happened.' He paused, then added slowly, 'And even if they find there is nothing wrong, they will share in any money Don Diego is offering.'

'The hell with that!' Mel roared, face ugly. 'You damn well make your checks! I ain't sharin' any money with no bunch of greasers.'

'You include me, eh, Mel?'

'Wipe that damn smile off your face! OK — I could stand to share with you if I had to but no one else, savvy? Where you gotta make your check?'

Dolfo gestured vaguely south. 'First, at a small rancho and cantina Don Diego does business with. On the edge of Indian country.'

'Pablito's? Makes his own *mescal*? Yeah, I know it.'

'We can pick up three or four *guerros* there. They will help us flush out this Taggart, and have no need to know about any bounty. I think it will save us a lot of time.'

Mel thought about it briefly, nodded, lifted his reins. 'Let's go. Just make sure these *guerros* don't shoot to kill. I want Taggart for myself.'

Dolfo nodded: that would be a problem to be faced when it arose. Mel or Don Diego: which would get Taggart?

*   *   *

To reach Don Diego Escalante's hacienda it needed a wide swing that would take him around San Antonio. Taggart had no doubt that the Mexican would have men there, watching for his return with Dolfo, and he did not want to be seen. Especially alone.

The trail took him through rough country, dry washes and crumbling gulches. His canteen was almost empty — as was his belly. His head throbbed and his thigh ached.

But he clutched the flatbow, and arrows rested in the rawhide-and-buckskin quiver slung across his back. Red Wing's body still lay undisturbed in the cave: the Kiowa had chosen his last resting-place himself and somehow it was devoid of vermin and other scavenging animals. He had not been gnawed or touched in any way. It made

Taggart feel kind of . . . creepy, and he wasted no time in collecting the bow and arrows and leaving the cave. And its silent occupant.

He hadn't seen any sign of Dolfo or Mel Wetherby but there had been a few dust devils that he took to be scattered riders. It could be they had called in help to track him down. So he made his sweep around San Antone as wide as he dared without using up too much time.

Then, suddenly, when he was riding through a narrow ravine with grey-green, dusted brush growing out of the walls, he glimpsed a splash of colour. Blue and what might have been dirty white or faded yellow. Sure not part of the scant vegetation. More like a man's shirt or neckerchief.

He dismounted behind a rock outcrop, took off his spurs and left them on the rock beside the ground-hitched horse, then started around and upwards, holding an arrow against the flat bowstave as he climbed carefully up the slope of the wall. As he drew closer he could see that he was right: a man wearing a blue shirt and yellow neckerchief was crouched with a rifle. He was side-on to Taggart and on the edge of a drop into a narrow cleft. But it would give him a good view of anyone riding through the ravine. Maybe he had heard Taggart's horse coming, for he was ready to shoot now and . . .

The man must have caught some movement out of the corner of his eye, for he suddenly swung towards Taggart, and brought the rifle up to his shoulder.

There was a thrumming sound and a *woosh*! and the man was transfixed by the arrow, through the centre of his chest. He reared up, clawing at the quivering shaft, dropping his rifle into the cleft. Then he tumbled in after it, body jamming several feet down.

Taggart swore; he would have liked to have got his hands on the man's guns. Then another rifle cracked from higher up the wall and lead streaked a trail of rockdust beside him. He dropped lower, fitting another arrow, as more lead raked his shelter. The man up there was anxious to get him and stood up so he could shoot better.

It was a bad mistake on his part. As the killer drew his bead, Taggart stepped out swiftly, the bow coming up, the string taut at full draw, the arrowhead all the way back to the bent wood, just touching his left hand where it gripped the stave. The shaft flashed and the man up there had only time to turn away in an effort to jump back before the arrow took him through the throat. He toppled back out of sight.

But the damage had been done: the rifle fire had attracted others. Taggart didn't recognize Dolfo or Mel Wetherby amongst the three riders who appeared on the top of the ravine; they were all strangers, hardcases by the looks of them. He didn't stay to see more, but jumped down to the next level and stumbled as they started shooting. Dust and rock chips exploded all around him as he ran, limping, for the outcrop where he had left the sorrel. He slung the bow across his back as he scooped up his spurs and leapt into the saddle. His horse snorted in protest at being interrupted in its browsing on the sparse grass but answered the thrust of his boot-heels against its flanks. Clint wheeled hard left and headed away from the ravine, as the guns above hammered away.

There was a large patch of brush stretching ahead on the side of a rise. Glancing over his shoulder, he saw that the pursuers had spread out and were racing to cut him off from this brush; they wanted to keep him out in the open where they could see what he was doing.

Taggart's horse was weary and he knew he wasn't going to make it to the brush that would give him cover. If he went left, one of the riders would angle in until he was within rifle range and then bring down his mount. Afoot, he wouldn't stand a chance.

The same hazard applied to the right

and, of course, there would be no point in trying to do an about-turn when the third rider was directly behind.

He deliberately slowed the horse.

He didn't do it all at once, tried to make it look as if exhaustion was the cause. He briefly heard a wild shout behind; at least one of the riders was convinced the sorrel was going down under him.

The three riders then swept in closer together, forcing him towards one side of the brush; it was where he wanted to go but he did his best to make it look just the opposite, pulling false starts, and sudden changes of direction.

They had some fun with him, shooting in front of the slowing mount. Taggart yanked the reins, making the horse shy away from the spurts of dust and gravel. He heard their laughter through the hot afternoon.

Then, when they grouped again and made it clear they were in charge here, he made a sharp turn, running the mount for the edge of the brush.

They didn't like it but they were in no hurry; they controlled that border of the brush now and even allowed him to reach the extreme outside. At a yell from one of the men, the trio charged deeper into the brush and began to cut through it, someone calling, 'Come on in, Taggart! We don't mind playin' a little hide-an'-go-seek!'

Taggart wheeled away into a small dry wash, the only place where he could take refuge. The trio started shooting, driving him in deeper, convinced he had signed his death warrant.

But it was too deep for them to see him dismount, pluck handfuls of dry grass and bundles of twigs from the scattered brush growing there. Like all cattlemen, he always carried a supply of rawhide strips for binding broken tools or the feet of troublesome mavericks. In seconds, Clint had two arrows with bundles of the dry tinder wrapped around the shafts just above the arrowheads.

He lit one, drew and aimed high, sending the arrow arcing up across the pulsing blue sky, leaving a thin white trail of smoke. The trio watched, puzzled at first. Then the wind of the arrow's passage fanned the flames and when it hit, fiery handfuls rained over a wide area of brush.

It was tinder-dry and ablaze in seconds, even before the second arrow landed over to the hunters' right and set more flames roaring as they wheeled their mounts that way.

Taggart worked fast, fired three more fire arrows and by then the entire hillside was on fire, choking smoke swirling up from the sotol and grease-wood in thick, roiling clouds, flames encircling the now frantic riders.

In the midst of this roaring ring of fire, the trio were shouting and scream-ing, fighting their terrified horses, trying to find a way out of the inferno.

Taggart mounted and rode around the base of the blazing hillside, knowing that Dolfo and Mel Wetherby would come riding in fast when they saw the fire.

By then, he would be screened by the choking pall of smoke and riding south towards Escalante's hacienda.

# 12

## US Marshal

It was a considerable shock to Clint Taggart when he rode his near-jaded horse down from the escarpment known as the Balcones, and saw a rider sitting squarely in the trail ahead, hands on his saddle horn.

There was no mistaking Mel Wetherby.

The big killer smiled coldly as Taggart hauled rein.

'Take you too long to unsling that there bow, Taggart. I'd put three bullets in you before you got started.' As he spoke his right hand moved swiftly and then Taggart was staring into the barrel of a cocked Colt. The gun jerked slightly to the right. 'If I didn't do it, Dolfo would . . . So shuck that bow now! Right now!'

Taggart hesitated only briefly, then unslung the bow and quiver, dropped them to the ground.

The tall Mexican, with his eye-patch looking more rakish than ever, walked his mount forward from among the tall boulders that stood beside the trail. He smiled amiably enough at the rancher, nodding.

'*Buenos dias*, Señor Taggart. You are surprised to see us, eh?'

Taggart stared back, nodded once. 'Guess I'm a blame fool. Figured I'd outsmarted you and those idiots who got their tails singed in the brush country. Forgot one thing: that you knew where I was headed all along. Didn't really matter if you caught up with me on the way down here, because I had to come this way eventually.'

'You're about as smart as the average lousy Ranger,' Mel said sourly, 'so I wouldn't feel too bad about it.'

'Been away from 'em for too long, I guess. Not used to trying to outsmart scramble-brained outlaws these days.'

Mel laughed harshly. 'Scramble-brained? *You're* the one under the gun!'

Taggart had to admit he was the foolish one here: so worried about Rachel, he had taken too many chances. He lifted his hands shoulder-high, flicking his gaze from Mel to the Mexican. 'You gonna fight over me now?' *Stirring things up — dangerously so.*

Dolfo's one eye glittered and he swung it quickly towards Wetherby who didn't take his gaze off the rancher.

'What's there to fight over? You're dead whatever happens, Taggart. Don Diego wants your head and I'm about ready to separate it from you.'

'There has been a change of plan, Mel!' the Mexican said quickly. 'I tried to tell you back there but you were too impatient to listen.'

'I heard you say you were gonna take in Taggart alive, but what's the difference? He dies anyway.'

'Don't shoot him!' Dolfo said bleakly

and there was a faint whispering sound as the big Le Mat slid into his hand. 'Don Diego has decided to torture him first. He has already sent Consuela to Denver to get Taggart's daughter.'

That brought Mel's head up with a snap. 'The hell you say! Didn't even know he had a daughter.'

'Taggart must suffer much before he dies. Don Diego will make him watch the child's death before finally giving orders to finish him.'

Mel frowned. 'His daughter's only a kid?'

Dolfo shrugged but Taggart, sick to his stomach, yet sensing something unexpected here, said quietly, 'Just eight years old, Mel.'

Wetherby pursed his lips, frowning more deeply. 'Aw, I dunno about this. I might've killed a kid or two in my time but it weren't meant to happen, just couldn't be avoided. I'm kinda leery of that kind of thing. I know you Mexes can cut a baby's throat without blinkin' an eye, specially if it's to do with family honour and stuff, but to make a man watch his own kid die.' He shook his head jerkily. 'Count me out of that stuff, Dolfo.'

'It is not for me to say, Mel. You must argue this with Don Diego himself.'

'The hell I will! I din' even like the sound of takin' Taggart's head off when me and Mitch first started lookin' for him. But after he killed Mitch I got myself to where I reckoned I could do it. Fact, I was lookin' forward to it. So, I think that's what we'll do: kill Taggart, and take his head back to Diego.'

Slowly, Dolfo said, 'This is not what I have been sent to do, Mel.'

'OK. So I do it, go back alone, tell Diego I haven't seen you, so I didn't know of the change of plan. I'll still collect my bounty and I won't feel so bad about Mitch bein' killed. You'll still keep your job and everyone'll be happy.' He looked at Taggart then and grinned tightly. ''Cept poor ol' Taggart, of course!'

Clint threw himself sideways out of

the saddle as Mel fired. The bullet missed but he felt its wind past his face as he dropped. The second shot hit his horse and the animal reared, whickering, pawing the air, forcing Taggart to roll swiftly out of reach of those hoofs.

Then the Le Mat thundered and Mel was picked up by the driving buckshot and flung out of his saddle. He landed awkwardly and some bone in his body, maybe his neck, made an audible crack. He lay still, blood flooding through his tattered shirt, his lower face pocked by some of the pellets.

The smoking pistol covered Taggart as he picked himself up out of the dust. Although he couldn't see the selector on the top of the backstrap, the rancher somehow knew that this time Dolfo had pushed it across to normal fire the instant the shot barrel had discharged. He glanced at his horse which had settled some and was trying to lick at the bullet burn across its shoulder. It didn't seem too serious.

Clint lifted his hands out from his

sides, looking up apprehensively into the Mexican's narrow face.

'If you make trouble, I will say that Mel shot you before I was able to stop him, Taggart,' the Mexican warned softly. 'I would rather we went in together, but I will take in your corpse if there is no other way.'

'Up to you, Dolfo.' The rancher's voice was edgy, his eyes restless, trying to gauge this devious Mexican's mood. 'But if I'm dead, you'll have to shoot Don Diego yourself — and that's not part of your plan, is it? You want me to do it, then you shoot me to make it look like you were just a mite slow protecting Escalante, maybe even shoot Consuela — fact, you'll have to shoot her.' Then his face and voice hardened. 'And just where would that leave Rachel?'

Dolfo grunted, his one eye staring disconcertingly. 'I wondered if you would see how things might go, Taggart. I must watch that I do not underestimate you . . . If I take you in alive now, you may well manage to convince Don Diego of my plans before I can stop you. It is a dilemma, no?'

'Well, that'd just be a chance you'd have to take. Like Mel said, whatever happens now, I'm gonna be a dead man. And I reckon I'll take as many of you scum with me as I can.'

Dolfo's face was pale now. He stared down at Mel's body and suddenly spat on it. '*Diablo's* curse upon him! It was all right until he showed up! Gringo scum!' The big pistol moved in his hand as he took a firmer grip and Taggart braced himself for a bullet. But Dolfo was still staring thoughtfully at him. 'Your child is what matters most to you, eh, Taggart?'

'Of course she does. Otherwise you'd be dead long since.'

'So. If I can guarantee Rachel's safety, you will . . . co-operate with me? Do as I say, kill Don Diego? Then we could all escape together, you, me and the child.'

'I think you're just talking off the top

of your head, but I'll go along with you, for now. Till I get the lie of things better. Depends on what you have in mind.'

The white teeth flashed in Dolfo's swarthy face. 'You will agree,' he said confidently. 'Because of the child.'

'I'll do a lot of things because of Rachel — but I won't agree to anything until you tell me how you figure you can guarantee her safety. Sounds like a mighty big chore to me.'

'We-ell — perhaps I know a little more than I told you previously, eh?'

He began to chuckle as he saw the bewilderment on the rancher's face.

'And perhaps I say it wrong. Perhaps I meant it is you who will have to guarantee Rachel's safety. Even if you know you will not live to see it!'

★　★　★

Buck Kirby knew he had to take Jimmy Morse's long telegraph message into Senior Captain Eadie without delay.

But Eadie was locked in conference with some US marshal who had arrived and demanded an urgent interview. He was a young, well-built feller, looked mighty healthy, like a man used to regular meals, and yet there was no softness about him. Well-dressed, he walked like a cat, that kind of easy tensioned-spring stride, alert, ready for instant action.

His eyes seemed cold to Kirby although he had barely glimpsed the man as he was directed to Eadie's office. Now he was about to find out just how cold those eyes could get when he was interrupted. He knocked perfunctorily on the door and opened it even before Eadie growled an irritable 'Come in.'

'Sorry to interrupt, Captain, but there's something you ought a see.' Kirby waved the message form and Eadie, looking bleak, lifted a hand and snapped his fingers.

The marshal watched silently as Buck passed the form to Eadie, who began to read. He glanced up once, then read quickly. He set down the form and said,

'Buck, meet US Marshal Beau Kimble, comes all the way from Washington — Captain of Company Buck Kirby, Kimble.'

The Ranger and the Marshal gripped hands briefly, firmly, gazes touching. As Kimble eased back in his chair, Eadie said, holding up the yellow telegraph form,

'Bit of a coincidence. Marshal's here about those guns we recovered from the border raid.' The captain looked at Kimble. 'Buck led that raid, together with an ex-Ranger who knew the country, feller named Clint Taggart.'

'I know the name. Rancher, isn't he? I was sidekick to Marshal Bronco Madigan before he disappeared. I believe he once spent a short time recuperating on Taggart's spread after some kind of fracas. Thought highly of Taggart.'

'I recollect that. What happened to Madigan?'

Kimble's face closed down a little. 'No one knows for sure. He'll likely turn up some day.'

'One tough *hombre*.'

'He was that. What's the coincidence, Captain?'

'In the fracas, Taggart killed Franco Escalante, and Diego's out to get Taggart for it. This wire from his ramrod says Escalante's kidnapped Taggart's daughter and is using her as a hostage to bring Taggart to him. Aims to kill 'em both.'

Kimble's eyes were on Kirby now and the Ranger Captain saw how alert they were: the man was ready for instant action.

'This helps us, Buck. I have a deportation notice for Diego Escalante, signed by the President's legal adviser.' Kimble tapped his shirt-pocket. 'We've had enough of him organizing his revolutionaries from inside the US and Mexico City's demanding we return him, anyway. We *know* damn well all the trouble he causes but he buys immunity because he's so blamed rich. But the President wants him out of Texas and back to Mexico pronto.' He paused before he added, 'No matter what we have to do to fix it. You know what I'm saying?'

Kirby nodded slowly, feeling a tightening in his belly. 'The . . . President of the United States is going to go along with . . . ?' He had to pause, couldn't say it out loud.

Kimble bored those now hard eyes into Buck and nodded gently. 'Whatever has to be done. He doesn't have to know details, just so long as it has at least the appearance of legality. We can't afford to alienate Mexico City because of one man — certainly not a man like Escalante. He's had more than his share of luck in the States.'

Kirby turned his head back and forth between the two men, spoke to Eadie: 'How does Jimmy Morse's wire help, Captain?'

Eadie gestured to Kimble. 'The Marshal's in charge here, Buck.'

Kimble said quietly, 'We know those guns were stolen by Escalante's men and you and your men kept them from reaching the revolutionaries — You recovered almost all of the weapons, still have them on Station here, I believe?'

He arched his eyebrows at Eadie who nodded. 'Army's sending in a troop to escort 'em back to where they belong next week.'

Kimble smiled faintly and leaned back in his chair, locking his fingers, hands across his chest. 'I'm confiscating ten or a dozen of those weapons, Buck.'

'I guess you got the authority.'

Kimble didn't even bother to acknowledge that. 'It's important, for appearances' sake — and no doubt for any legal appeal Escalante might make against his deportation. He's a dead man, of course, once he steps into Mexico. If we're able to show guns that match the description and serial numbers of some of those stolen from the Arlington Armoury were found in Diego's possession . . .

by you and your Rangers . . . '

He just looked steadily at Kirby who, after a slight hesitation, nodded. 'I . . . think I see. And if Escalante could also be charged with kidnapping, or the murder of Taggart's daughter, that would sort of clinch the whole deal.'

Kimble smiled at Eadie. 'I want this man and his company to help me on this, Captain.'

'Reckon that can be arranged. You came in to ask permission to help Taggart rescue his daughter, I take it, Buck?'

'Yessir. I mean, once a Ranger and all that. And Clint did risk his life to set up that border ambush for us.'

Eadie lifted a hand slightly. 'You don't need to convince me it's the thing to do. I think I can turn this whole business over to you, Marshal Kimble. You just ask for whatever you want. Buck'll see to it.'

Beau Kimble stood, hitching at his gunbelt and set his expensive-looking hat squarely on his head.

'We'll start getting this organized, Buck. Seems to me like it's taken on an extra urgency if we're going to save that little girl.'

Kirby held the door, watching the young lawman closely.

'That'll be the Rangers' first concern, Marshal.'

Kimble acknowledged that with a slight pause as he stepped past Kirby.

'We'll all try to make the entire operation a success, Buck. But there are several things here that *must* be done, some of more importance than any others . . . *Any* others, Buck. No matter who gets hurt. You understand?'

As Kirby closed the door after him, he couldn't help thinking,

*He might look a mite spoiled on the outside, but some of Madigan's hardness has sure rubbed off on this feller.*

# 13

## Rangers True

It was going to be a mighty delicate moment and Taggart wondered how Dolfo was going to manage it.

Taggart's six-gun had to be loaded before they approached the hacienda and went inside where they would be taken to Don Diego. But once Taggart had bullets in his guns, the tall Mexican would no longer be able to relax: he would be in mortal danger. Perhaps he was going to depend on Taggart deciding that he would need Dolfo to get him safely to Escalante — and away afterwards.

'We are expected, of course, *amigo*,' Dolfo said suddenly as they approached what Taggart figured must be the last mountain between them and the estancia. As the rancher's head turned towards him Dolfo smiled widely. 'When I made my check-in at San Antonio, I sent orders that as soon as we come within range, you are to be covered with a rifle every moment of our approach. At the first sign of hostile movement you are to be shot.'

Taggart almost smiled. 'Aw, now, Dolfo, you disappoint me. You mean you won't trust me once my gun's loaded?'

'I apologize, naturally, if your feelings are hurt, Señor Taggart,' the Mexican told him sardonically, 'but I can think of no other way. We will stop in a small arroyo before we ride up and across the last clear stretch to the *rancho*.'

Taggart didn't bother to answer; the Mexican had shown him once again that he had details already planned well ahead. He remembered how he had told Mel Wetherby that he had been too long away from the Rangers, that he was no longer thinking like one, seeing and examining every kind of possible danger. No doubt Dolfo was trading on this, too.

Clint avoided dwelling on Rachel's future; he supposed she was already with Don Diego and he knew she would come to no harm until he faced the hidalgo. That was when he would need every scrap of nerve and instant reaction he could muster.

Perhaps Dolfo already knew this and was counting on Taggart's co-operation until the moment they were face to face with Escalante.

Rachel would be in plenty of danger in that office with bullets flying in the enclosed area. But there was no way out of it that he could see. He intended to kill Escalante: there was no choice. The man was mad, a sadist, ready and willing to murder Rachel. He had to be killed, and Clint would relish the chance to do it. But it was at the very moment that his bullet cut Escalante down that the real danger would start for the child.

Dolfo would try to kill Taggart. Consuela was an unknown at the moment; she seemed fanatical from what Dolfo had told him, although the man could be deliberately exaggerating. He hoped he was!

Could she, *would* she, try to harm Rachel the moment her father was shot down? So many damn things to think about! His heart seemed to somersault in his chest. God Almighty! He abruptly realized it wasn't that he had forgotten his Ranger training, or that he was easy to outsmart by these lawbreakers: it was because of Rachel! She was going to be in the thick of it all, in more deadly danger than she ever should know in her entire life, if she lived to be a hundred!

Because of *him*, and some twist of fate that had opposed him to Franco Escalante at the river, unknown machinations had brought his daughter into this life-threatening situation. That was what was blunting his ability to find a safe way out of this.

'We stop here.'

Dolfo's words were like a whiplash, sharp, cutting, and Clint knew the tall

Mexican was on edge, too. *Make a note of that!* Dolfo had as much, maybe more, to lose than Taggart himself and his emotions must be running mighty high.

They had reached the arroyo; it was time for Taggart to load his Colt. Dolfo had the rancher's gun-rig hanging from his saddle horn, now he motioned to Taggart to dismount, stretch out face down on the ground and place his hands in his hip-pockets.

Taggart obeyed and then Dolfo took the rancher's Colt, thumbed two shells only from the cartridge loops and loaded them into the six-gun's cylinder. He snapped it closed and rammed it into the holster. Then he unslung the rig from the saddle horn and tossed it into a bush several feet away.

Dolfo drew his large Le Mat and flicked the lever across to the shot barrel, gesturing with a jerk of the gun for Taggart to get to his feet.

'You will take the rig down with one hand and then buckle it on, facing me, *señor*. After that we will ride in, you first. I will be right behind you.' He smiled then. 'Actually a little to one side — you will recall I said you would be covered with a rifle from the *rancho* gatehouse?'

'I haven't forgotten,' Taggart said moodily. 'Let's get started.'

Dolfo nodded, gestured with his pistol and, as Taggart settled in the saddle, there came a scattering of wild yells and a crash of gunfire from the direction of the *estancia* hidden by the rising land beyond the arroyo.

Followed by a rumbling explosion.

'Dynamite,' Taggart said slowly, watching the Mexican very closely now. But the big gun did not waver.

'I think we must check the hacienda,' Dolfo said. 'Go!'

Taggart rode ahead, up and out of the arroyo. The *rancho* was half a mile away. The big wooden entrance gates under their adobe arch lay shattered, hanging precariously from the hinges. Smoke swirled, and through the fog a dozen or more riders crowded through the gateway, guns hammering.

He could see running *vaqueros* beyond, some shooting back at the raiders, others being ridden down or shot as they ran.

'*Dios!* Who are they?'

Without thinking about it, Taggart, still watching, answered, 'Ranger troop . . .'

He snapped his head back instantly, hand starting towards his gun butt. He froze, under the yawning muzzles of the Le Mat. Above the big pistol, Dolfo's face was ashen, his mouth tight, nostrils pinched and the solitary eye half-closed.

'Now you will never find out the fate of your daughter!' he said in little above a harsh whisper.

Taggart straightened a little in the saddle. 'Not taking any chances, eh, Dolfo? Can't afford to take me in alive now.'

'You know I can not.'

'Yeah, I know. I figured you'd try to kill me sometime, but I reckoned you'd give me the shot barrel on that damn cannon, not just a bullet.'

'I have already chosen the big barrel . . . '

Dolfo instinctively glanced down to make sure the lever was pushed to the left for the shot barrel.

In that split second he died.

Taggart's Colt swept up and he drove both bullets into the tall Mexican. They lifted Dolfo out of the saddle and before he hit the ground Taggart was reloading the smoking Colt with cartridges from his belt loops.

As soon as he had two thumbed home he snapped the loading gate closed. He cocked the hammer but Dolfo was unmoving, sprawled on his back, his Le Mat jammed under one hip, still gripped in the hand trapped beneath his body.

Taggart opened the loading gate again and filled the cylinder, watching the hacienda.

He loaded the rifle, thinking that Jimmy Morse's wire must have reached

Buck Kirby all right. He hadn't expected an all-out raid on Escalante's *estacia* but hoped that Kirby might at least have had a couple of men watching for his arrival.

Now it sounded like the Little Big Horn with all the shooting and shouting and screams of mortally wounded men. Smoke from the dynamite blast that had shattered the main gates was lifting slowly now and he saw some of the battle through the archway: running men, blazing guns, tumbling bodies.

Holding the fully loaded Winchester, he spurred the mount towards the scene of the battle, heart hammering as he wondered whether Rachel was somewhere in there, menaced by flying lead — or something worse, in the shape of a crazed Escalante — or Consuela.

★　★　★

After the dynamite blasted the gates Kirby's men charged full tilt, coming out of the choking, blinding smoke like raging centaurs. The Mexicans inside, those who hadn't been killed or stunned by the blast, were still gathering their senses as the Rangers' guns cut them down. Some fired back from the main house and horses whickered in terror and hurt, going down and throwing their riders.

Marshal Kimble had his rifle butt pressed into his right hip, working lever and trigger, the muzzle sweeping in a slow, deadly arc, finding a target with almost every shot.

Kirby kept close to two men who carried a long canvas-wrapped bundle between them. The Ranger captain held a blazing six-gun in each hand, triggered at a man at the top of a set of tiled stairs. As the body fell he gestured for the two Rangers to follow him and sprinted up the stairs.

They led to a paved gallery and, at the far end, two Mexicans were kneeling, one with a rifle, the other with a shotgun. Kirby and his men dived for the floor, the bundle striking heavily as the shotgun blasted. One of the Rangers reeled violently, half-lifted to slam against the whitewashed adobe arch support. His blood smeared the wall and Kirby, on his belly, fired both guns. The shotgunner staggered but his sidekick got off two more shots before disappearing around the corner. The wounded shotgunner, holding his side, half-doubled over, staggered after him.

Kirby glanced at his man, saw that the buckshot had blown out the Ranger's ribs and there was no hope for him. He snapped at the other man and they lifted the bundle between them, Kirby using only one hand, a six-gun cocked in the other.

At the end of the gallery they approached warily but no one was waiting at the other side. A door was half-open, moving slightly, but the drops of fresh blood from the wounded shotgunner led past the door and on down the passage. Kirby looked closely at the door and a small number-plate fixed to it: 6. He nodded, motioned for his helper to stand the bundle against the wall, then pushed the door open warily. Inside, a small fat man was stuffing papers into a briefcase. He spun round now, wild-eyed. He thrust both hands into the air when he saw the Ranger. Guns hammered in other parts of the building and there was a lot of yelling.

'All right, *amigo*, do as you're told and you won't come to any harm. *Comprendes?*'

The terrified man's bladder had emptied and there was a spreading dark patch down the front of his trousers. But he seemed uncaring about it and nodded that he would co-operate with Kirby.

'Brazos,' Kirby called. 'Drag that bundle in here. You, friend, I want you to open that big oak cupboard in the corner. *That* one. Don't play dumb or you'll have more than hot piss messin' up your clothes.'

The man was shaking badly, fumbled

keys on a ring that held at least a dozen. He opened the cupboard door. It contained cardboard file folders, a couple of old valises bulging with papers, a surveyor's theodolite on a tripod and other miscellaneous gear. Kirby smiled at Brazos as the man struggled with the canvas-wrapped bundle.

'Plenty of room.'

Brazos lumbered across, pushed and puffed and jammed the long bundle into the cupboard. Kirby closed the door and ordered the little man to lock it again. Then he took the key-ring, walked to the door and hurled it out into the plaza below where the fighting was slowing now. He glimpsed several Mexicans, unarmed and with hands thrust into the air under the guns of powder-smeared Rangers.

The fat man looked puzzled and Kirby grinned. 'Go find Kimble,' he told Brazos. 'And keep an eye out for Taggart's kid. Hey, *amigo*, you'd better sit down before you collapse. Get in there behind your desk and don't move, OK?'

The little man was on the verge of fainting and obeyed. It was several minutes before Brazos returned with Beau Kimble in tow. The marshal had a little blood splashed on his clothes, a smear over one cheek. His eyes were squinted, his nostrils moist, like a man who had breathed too much gunsmoke. 'What have we here, Buck?' Kimble gestured to the wilting Mexican.

'Escalante's clerk, I guess. He refuses to open that big cupboard and I can't find any keys.' He glared at the little man who began to protest, but Buck talked over any words he might have uttered. 'Figured it'd be best if you were on hand to witness my opening the cupboard. Just in case it's somethin' that has to be used in court later . . . '

'Good idea, Buck,' Kimble said, deadpan. 'Let's see what's in there that he doesn't want us to find.'

Brazos had his rifle and at a nod from Kirby, stepped forward and began battering at the panelled doors with the heavy brass buttplate. The little Mexican made a gasping sound, gripped the arms of his chair tightly but said nothing as the oak splintered. In moments, the doors sagged and Brazos tore them off the hinges, flinging them aside.

'Looks like a lot of junk,' Marshal Kimble opined. 'Could be just a cover, though. What's in that bundle?'

Brazos struggled to drag out the canvas-wrapped bundle he had placed inside only minutes before. He let it fall. It made a dull, clunking sound. Kirby knelt and used his jack-knife to cut the rope bindings. He threw back the canvas and the Rangers and Kimble looked suitably surprised.

'Well — will you look at that now?' Buck Kirby said as if he had never seer the dozen new Sharps falling-blc rifles before. 'Looks like they coul' part of the haul from the Arl' Armory up north, Marshal.'

'If the serial numbers match

the stolen guns,' Kimble said, turning towards the fat little Mexican, 'this'll get Escalante deported, if not hung . . . '

But the clerk had slid down out of the chair and was sprawled unconsious half-under his desk. Kimble grunted.

'All right. No need for any more play-acting. Let's go see if Escalante can explain this away.'

Kirby smiled crookedly and Brazos gave a brief guffaw. Then the trio froze as a big shape filled the doorway.

'To hell with your guns and Escalante. Has anyone seen my daughter?'

Taggart, wild-eyed, stood there, boots a little apart, a smoking Colt in one hand, rifle dangling from the other.

An avenging angel ready to strike.

Kimble cleared his throat. 'I'm a US marshal — You must be Taggart. Escalante's a prisoner in his main office. But I'm sorry to tell you that there's been no sign of your little girl anywhere, Taggart.'

★  ★  ★

Escalante was literally foaming at the mouth. He was being guarded by two hard-eyed, weary Rangers. Kirby and the others arrived and both Rangers nodded briefly as they recognized Taggart. But the rancher only had eyes for Don Diego who struggled constantly against the grips of the big Rangers. They held him mostly erect in front of a huge, ornately carved desk. Taggart strode forward and backhanded Escalante, blood mixing with the cream-coloured foam dribbling from his cruel mouth.

Kimble and Kirby both stepped up to the rancher and reached for him. He shook them off, eyes blazing.

'You do what you have to. Frame him, plant evidence on him, throw him down the stairs and say he tripped. But do it after I've had five minutes with him — alone.'

Kirby looked sympathetic but Kimble shook his head slowly. 'Taggart, I c understand how you must feel a' your little girl — '

'Why? You got one, too?'

'No, but — '

'Then you understand nothing! I'm not a Ranger any more. You can't tell me what to do, Kimble. I just want — '

'I *know* what you want. And I'd admire to give you your five minutes alone with this snake — but there're a lot bigger things here than a kidnapping, though I can understand how you would contest that.'

Suddenly, Taggart spun, his Colt blurring out of leather and he fired. Escalante screamed and bucked and the Rangers, startled, released his arms. He fell, writhing and screaming, his right foot shattered, bones and torn flesh erupting through the bullet-ravaged shoe. He threw up violently on to the expensive carpet, unable to contain himself for the excruciating pain.

Kirby grabbed for Taggart's gun hand but Kimble merely pressed the muzzle of his Colt into the raging rancher's spine. 'I won't kill you, Taggart — unless I have to. But I can leave you in a lot of pain if you don't holster that six-gun and *keep* it holstered.'

Taggart, breath hissing through pinched nostrils, glared pure hatred at Kimble. It was so strong that the marshal even felt a little blood drain from his face.

'Come on, Taggart. You were a lawman once. You know how it works.' In a low voice, he added, 'We've got Escalante right where we want him. I have a signed, presidential deportation order. We've . . . arranged evidence now that makes it inevitable that Diego *will* be deported. There will be no appeal. The Mexicans are waiting on the other side of the Rio. Escalante's finished, Taggart. He has no future.'

Taggart slowly holstered his Colt but the intensity of his stare did not diminish. 'I don't care about his future. It's Rachel's I want to ensure — and if that son of a bitch doesn't tell me where she is — '

'I'll volunteer to shoot his other foot,' Buck Kirby said suddenly, startling them.

Kimble frowned. 'By God, Buck, you sound as if you mean that!'

''Course I damn well mean it! Taggart used to be in my company. Rangers don't forget their pards, Marshal.' There was a slight twist to his mouth as he flicked his gaze to Taggart. 'Even if they're sometimes seen as a possible threat to an officer, via promotion.'

Taggart's face didn't change but he nodded briefly.

Kimble suddenly sighed. 'All right. Escalante's finished, nothing can change that. I'm going outside to smoke a cigarillo along the other end of the gallery, out of earshot. I'll be back in about five minutes.' He moved to the door as he was speaking, gave them a quick on-off smile, and closed it after him.

Taggart turned back to the sobbing Escalante who was tenderly holding his mangled foot. The man looked up at the rancher with smouldering black eyes. 'I will — burn in — hell — before I tell you — anything!'

Taggart nodded casually. 'Yeah, I

know how it works with you old hidalgos, Escalante. All that honour and pride and hatred for the gringo just spilling out of you. Well, I can match all that, Diego — with my love for my daughter. I'm not generally a cruel man but I'm telling you now, you won't have to wait to go to Hell to suffer the tortures of the damned. I'm standin' in for Old Nick, right here, right now.'

He drew his Colt and placed the muzzle on top of the Mexican's left foot. 'I want you to tell me where Rachel is — *now!*'

The hammer made a loud sound as it cocked and Buck Kirby felt a tingle as a cold shiver ran down his spine.

★　★　★

The train came limping in to the crowded depot on the north side of San Antonio.

It still had some mud plastered on the locomotive, the roof over the driving-cab, and along the sides of the two passenger-cars. According to Escalante it had been delayed by a mudslide and there were passengers hanging out of the windows, waving and calling to anxious friends and relatives who had expected the train the day previously.

Standing just inside the ticket-office, with Buck Kirby, Taggart raked his gaze along the passenger cars. He stiffened suddenly and Kirby said, 'You see her?'

'No. Not Rachel. But I think that must be Consuela. She's expecting to be met by the looks of it.'

'Well, she will be.'

'Don't move, Buck! I want to make sure Rachel's with her and safe. Consuela's stepping down but I can't see for the crowds, goddamnit!'

'Easy! There's nothin' she can do now. Not here.'

Taggart merely looked at the Ranger and Kirby dropped his gaze. They had no idea what this Mexican girl was capable of . . . Hell, it would be a downright calamity if something terrible happened to the child at this stage.

Taggart was moving. He lunged out of the ticket-office, shoving protesting folk out of the way in his hurry. Kirby swore softly as he tried to follow but was blocked by the milling crowds.

Then Taggart stopped dead. Consuela, dressed in a travel-creased blue dress, her small hat somewhat askew, was straining to see past the jostling passengers and those who came to meet them. She saw him. She stared briefly, turned and pulled a startled child out from behind her voluminous skirts, holding the small hand tightly.

She had grown, Taggart thought, in size and beauty. He felt a lurch in his heart: My God! She was Lorene in miniature! Same hair, same eyes, same smile, flashing as she saw him.

'*Daddy!*'

The small voice, filled with pleasure and excitement, reached him above the hubbub of the siding. He didn't move. Because now Rachel was looking up puzzledly into Consuela's beautiful face, struggling to pull her small hand

245

free of the Mexican girl's tight grip. 'Consuela! It's Daddy! You said I could go to him as soon as we found him . . .'

'I am sorry, little one. Wait.' Consuela tightened her grip as she held Taggart's gaze. 'So — you are him! My brother's killer!'

'Let the child go, Consuela,' Taggart said hoarsely.

'She is a lovely child. We have become good friends. Such nice manners, fine looks, excited with her love for you and the anticipation of seeing you again. So full of *life*! I am truly sorry she must witness your . . . death!'

She pushed the struggling child to one side, and fired a double-barrelled Deringer through the side of her silk handbag. It was fast, so fast and unexpected that Taggart's right hand had just closed around his gun butt when he felt the ball smash into his side. He staggered, the crowd scattering. The child screamed, terrified, impassioned.

'*Daddeeee!*'

Then Kirby's Colt barked beside the rancher, briefly deafening him. Clint swayed, dropping to one knee. He let his gun fall back into the holster. There would be no need for it now. Consuela was down, blood on her bodice, face ghastly white, body very still.

'Damn! Only meant to wing her,' said Kirby shaking his head regretfully. 'But Rachel's safe now, anyway.'

Tears streaming down her small face, Rachel ran towards Taggart, blond hair streaming. He pressed one hand into his bleeding side, struggling to his feet. Her face suddenly cleared, eyes bright now with pleasure as she saw he was all right.

He smiled despite the pain and opened his arms to welcome her.

## THE END

We do hope that you have enjoyed reading this large print book.

Did you know that all of our titles are available for purchase?

We publish a wide range of high quality large print books including:
**Romances, Mysteries, Classics
General Fiction
Non Fiction and Westerns**

Special interest titles available in large print are:
**The Little Oxford Dictionary
Music Book, Song Book
Hymn Book, Service Book**

Also available from us courtesy of Oxford University Press:
**Young Readers' Dictionary
(large print edition)
Young Readers' Thesaurus
(large print edition)**

For further information or a free brochure, please contact us at:
**Ulverscroft Large Print Books Ltd.,
The Green, Bradgate Road, Anstey,
Leicester, LE7 7FU, England.
Tel:** (00 44) **0116 236 4325
Fax:** (00 44) **0116 234 0205**

# MASSACRE AT BLUFF POINT

## I. J. Parnham

Ethan Craig has only just started working for Sam Pringle's outfit when Ansel Stark's bandits bushwhack the men at Bluff Point. Ethan's new colleagues are gunned down in cold blood and he vows revenge. But Ethan's manhunt never gets underway — Sheriff Henry Fisher arrests him and he's accused of being a member of the very gang he'd sworn to track down! With nobody believing his innocence and a ruthless bandit to catch, can Ethan ever hope to succeed?